Waking Up Dead

An Endless Mountains Ghost Story

Regge Episale

ISBN-13: 978-1469953007

ISBN-10: 1469953005

DEDICATION

To Angela for giving me Deidra Shay. To Frank for giving me the challenge to write this story. To both for believing in me.

ACKNOWLEDGMENTS

Like raising children, writing a book takes a village. I have a very special village. Thank you so much to Frank and Angela for your never-ending faith in my ability to do this, and for the hours you spend listening to me think. Thank you, Sarah and Kassie, for being willing to read and edit. Thank you, Mike, for my lovely office where I can write. Thank you, Darla and Morgan, for that wonderful picture on the cover, and to Darlene for answering medical questions. A special thank you to my sister, Faye, for being constantly by my side, in my corner; for reading, editing and sharing all of those long, long conversations over coffee. Thank you, also, for sharing your ghosts with me.

CHAPTER 1

Later, much later, Jesse would look back and wonder how that day could have seemed so normal right up until the moment it exploded. She would search for signs, for premonitions, but there were none. It was just another day until it wasn't.

Brian followed Jesse's diminutive form around the liquor store with his hands in his pockets, the bored look on his face speaking volumes. Jesse did her best to ignore him but couldn't deny her hurt and aggravation. She was sorry she'd asked him along. Any chance that he'd be sociable and make an attempt to get to know Deidra better was obviously out of the question.

"You could at least try to enjoy your time with me," she suggested. To her own disgust her voice came out in a whine rather than the bantering tone she was going for. She sighed and gave up the attempt. "I'll finish up here and buy you dinner and a drink as a consolation prize," she snapped. "At least with Deidra in town you won't be stuck with me anymore this week."

Brian raised his eyebrows and sent a sideways glance at her, a smile that bordered on a smirk tilting his lips just the slightest. "I take it I'm being a jerk."

"Oh really? I hadn't noticed," she quipped but as always a smile on his lips put a smile on hers and she relaxed. "I just don't understand what you dislike so much about Deidra. She's my best friend."

"She's just ... never mind. I am being a jerk; probably jealous that she's going to get all of your time while she's here. I'll be nice, okay? Dinner is on me if you promise to stop being pissed off."

Jesse had to stretch in order to get her hands around his neck so she could pull his face down to hers. "Lobster," she said, "at Coopers."

"Stiff price," he groaned but the quick kiss and full smile told Jesse he was over his funk.

Deidra answered yet another curtain call to hoots and wolf-whistles. She sauntered back onto the stage of "Achilles Heel" and curtsied as low as she dared in order to give the audience yet another long look at the

4

generous bosom her character, Adele, had used to lure all kinds of men into romantic dalliances throughout the play.

As she straightened up, Deidra tossed her head, sending long black curls flying. It was a move she knew looked sexual but which really served to hide the perspiration that wanted to matt her hair down flat. The stage lights were unbearably hot.

She watched for signs that people were getting bored—tired of waiting for the finale they had heard so much about. At the very moment some started to reach for their coats she turned away from them, sauntered toward the back of the stage, smiled back over her shoulder and mooned the audience.

Her black dress flipped up to expose three inch heels, impossibly long legs and an ample butt covered in black lace panties. On one generous cheek a large red heart flashed on and off. Deidra/Adele smiled, licked her top lip, crooked her finger as if beckoning someone and watched men's faces flush while they adjusted coats or programs or anything they could find to cover their collective crotch. The audience roared their appreciation as the applause started all over again.

Deidra would have taken another bow but the last bus to Scranton left at eleven PM and she had promised Jesse she'd catch it. She grabbed her coat and raced for the door, nearly running over her agent. "Deidra, just a minute …"

"Gotta run—really."

Sandy pushed a large manila envelope into her hands before waving her on. "For the bus ride," she said. "It's a script with your name on it."

Deidra nodded that she understood and ran. She spun through the door and danced down the steps into Connor's arms. As tall as she was, he was even taller. He lifted her into the air and spun her around. She struggled back to her feet as she pushed him away, but not before she felt a ring slide on to her left hand.

Connor backed away and popped the cork from a bottle of champagne. She grabbed his arm as she waved down the nearest taxi. "Port Authority—I'm late!" she told the driver.

Connor sighed in exasperation. "Could you at least *look* at your left hand? Say yes or no? Maybe you can postpone your trip?"

Deidra squealed as she held her hand up to the city lights. She climbed onto Connor's lap and pulled him close. "Of course I'm saying 'yes'! Oh, Connor, this is just too much!" She reached inside his suit jacket and pulled up his shirt, crushing her chest against his bare chest and giggling. Connor caught the taxi driver's eyes in the rearview mirror and grinned. The driver turned his face back to the road.

"I wish you weren't going," Connor groaned into her neck.

"But you're joining me in three days, right? Think of all the fun we'll have when you've had a chance to miss me." Deidra ran her tongue up the sensitive muscle of his neck and jumped out of his reach when he grabbed for her. "It's a promise," she laughed.

At Port Authority, Deidra ran down the three sets of steps and waved her ticket under the nose of the startled bus driver. "I can't wait to tell Jesse!" She swung up the steps and onto the bus, stopping to throw a kiss in Connor's direction.

"I'm going to *hate* your Jesse!" Connor called after her. "I am officially jealous!"

She slipped into a seat, pulled the window open and blew him kisses, which he caught and blew back to her until the rest of the passengers were staring— some with frowns of disapproval or discomfort and others with suggestive grins.

Deidra fell asleep, grateful for the air rushing through the window, her large diamond flashing on her long fingers, which trailed the bus floor.

She didn't know she was sleeping. She didn't know when a stray bullet, fired as a warning over the head of a fleeing suspect by a part-time police officer in Mount Pocono, Pennsylvania, entered the open window. She didn't know when it entered her heart and stopped it, immediately and completely.

At one-thirty AM, Jesse jerked awake in the car, a knife-like pain startling a scream from her. Next to her, Brian startled awake. "What's wrong?"

The pain left as suddenly as it had arrived. "Nothing. Go back to sleep. She won't be here for another half-hour." Brian patted her hand and dozed, his head propped against the window.

Jesse waited for Deidra's bus to arrive, a nagging worry at the back of her mind. Fog was settling in. She absently rubbed at the spot where pain had exploded so suddenly and then disappeared. A bottle of champagne and a liter of Jack Daniels waited in the back seat. Jack Daniels was Deidra's drink; no celebration would be complete without it.

The bus was late, crawling through fog and into the terminal at two o'clock. Jesse jumped from the car and paced back and forth while late-night passengers inched down the steps, collected their luggage and disappeared. Jesse knew Deidra would be the last one off; she hated being jostled. Minutes dragged by until the platform was empty, but still no Deidra. While the bus drivers chatted comfortably under the station lights, Jesse went searching. She walked the length of the bus, hopping up to peer through the windows over her head.

"Miss, please step away from the bus." Jesse startled.

"Sorry. I'm just looking for my friend. This is the last bus from New York, right?"

The driver sighed loudly and disengaged himself from his friends. "The next one comes in at three-ten," he said as he walked toward her. For a moment Jesse thought he might grab her arm and drag her away. "All of the passengers for this stop have gotten off."

"No, they haven't," Jesse insisted. "Maybe she's asleep." She turned away from him and sped up, walking briskly next to the bus and hopping up to see through the windows. She certainly hoped Deidra hadn't missed the eleven o'clock bus, but stranger things had happened.

"Then we'll find her when we do the check," the driver said sharply. "You can't be here right now."

Jesse continued to walk, the driver sighing in exasperation behind her.

"Please ...," he repeated.

But Jesse could see Deidra and pointed, laughing. "I'll just wake her up and be gone. She's a heavy sleeper."

"You can't board the bus!" but Jesse had already hurried up the few steps to the door and scampered down the aisle.

"Deidra! Wake up! You're getting me in trouble!" Jesse reached out to shake Deidra's shoulder. "Come on, Lazy Bones! You're here!" Deidra's body fell awkwardly forward, her head striking against the back of the seat in front of her. "Deidra?"

Jesse knew right then, just like that, that Deidra wasn't going to wake up. A long shuddering cry flew from her throat as the bus driver reached her and put a hand on her shoulder. "Miss, please step back."

"No!" Jesse screamed. "Deidra! Deidra, wake up!" She grabbed Deidra's hand, that long beautiful hand that hung over the side of the seat and sparkled with the new diamond. She pulled hard. "Deidra, stop scaring me! Wake up!"

Jesse hung on to Deidra's hand and sobbed. The driver put his arm around her shoulders and pulled, at first gently and then more urgently as another driver came to his aid. "No! No! No!" she screamed over and over.

Her screams mingled with and were lost in the wail of sirens, as police cars streamed into the area around the station. Two officers grabbed Jesse on either side and pulled her away, giving up on gentle urging and simply jerking her back until she lost contact with Deidra's fingers.

"You have to leave!" one shouted. Jesse clung to Deidra. As the officer pulled her away, the diamond ring slipped off of Deidra's finger and stayed in Jesse's clutched fist.

If Deidra Shay had known she was dead, she might have made different choices. But that's the nice thing about not knowing you're dead—it doesn't really worry you that much—not at first, anyway. She felt the ring slip away and grabbed for it. "Jesse? What are you doing? Hey!" But Jesse was pulled from the bus, unknowingly taking the diamond with her, and taking Deidra, too.

CHAPTER 2

Deidra was terribly, terribly cold, and something was wrong with her brain. She couldn't remember getting off the bus. She couldn't remember getting here. She did remember she was on her way to see Jesse, and here she was, rummaging through Jesse's room, searching for the sweater she had left behind months ago.

Jesse was acting very, very strange. Deidra wanted to talk about her new play, the standing ovation, the diamond Connor had slipped onto her finger in the middle of Houston Street. She wanted girl talk. She wanted to gossip and laugh and celebrate with shots of whiskey like they always did but Jesse, her best friend and partner in crime, was sleeping; sleeping like there was nothing going on at all. And it was so cold.

Jesse was sleeping with the help of half of the bottle of Jack that was meant for Deidra. Now she was as dead to the world as her best friend, and maybe more so. After all, Deidra knew she was confused and cold. Jesse, on the other hand, had intentionally used alcohol to kill the pain in her heart. It had taken a lot of whiskey to get her passed out and free of thought. Her breath still wobbled into her pillow, catching in soft sobs as she slept. Her eyes were swollen from crying, her hair wet plaster against her cheeks. Jesse knew very well that Deidra was dead. She had seen the body.

Jesse's brain struggled to consciousness as a sweatshirt landed on her feet. In the dark room a whisper of soft objects falling registered in Jesse's whiskey induced fog. *Brian?* But no, Brian had left before she went to bed. Fear paralyzed her. She could make out a figure in the filtered light of the corner street lamp—a shadow at the side of the bed. Someone was in the room. As Jesse watched, the shadowy form picked up a towel and tossed it. It hit the wall, falling to the floor with a soft *whomp*. Jesse lay absolutely still, holding her breath. She knew holding her breath was childish and useless but couldn't stop herself. As a little girl she had held her breath to keep the boogie man from finding her; now she had a real boogie man, and was holding it in earnest.

"I'm so cold. I'm just so cold." Deidra muttered.

"Deidra?" The name stuck in Jesse's throat. It couldn't be Deidra—but it was. Jesse could recognize her now. The long dark hair, the six feet of shapely woman with that slight rounding in the shoulders. Relief. "Deidra? Oh my God! They said you were dead!"

Deidra sat on edge of the bed. Jesse could feel the mattress react to new weight. Was that possible? If she were a ghost that wouldn't be possible, would it? It couldn't be. "Deidra!" Jesse started to laugh. "It's you! It's really you! Oh my God, I'm losing my mind. I honestly thought you were dead." She could hear herself rambling but couldn't stop. *I'm hysterical*, she thought. *This is what it means to be hysterical.* "Did I oversleep? It must have been a terrible, terrible nightmare. You wouldn't believe it. Oh, Deidra, how did you get here?" Jesse reached out her arms to draw Deidra into a hug and then froze.

Deidra picked up her sweater from the edge of the bed and put it on. "I'm so cold. I'm just so cold," she said.

As Jesse watched, time rewound. Deidra picked up her sweater from the edge of the bed and pulled it tightly around her shivering shoulders. "I'm so cold. I'm just so cold," she said.

And then she did it again.

Without a thought, Jesse pulled her own blankets up and reached out to wrap Deidra in their warmth—but Deidra was gone.

"I saw her." Jesse wrapped her hands around the coffee mug. She wondered how hard she could squeeze without breaking it. Probably hard—it was stoneware, after all. She watched her own knuckles turn white to avoid watching Brian study her. He was running out of patience, but she needed him to believe her. "I didn't just see her. I watched her throw my clothes around the room until she found her sweater. And then I watched her put the sweater on about a dozen times."

"I know that's what you think." Brian's voice wavered between annoyed and sympathetic. It came out very soft, very slow, and very distinct, like he was lecturing a child who was having trouble understanding, and thus obeying. "You were drunk. You were traumatized. You were dreaming. It's only

15

natural." He put his arm around her shoulders, stepping back as Jesse shrugged it off.

Brian's lips thinned without his even knowing it. He leaned away from her, studying the skeletal thinness of her, the light brown hair, the tiny, almost childlike features. It was the tininess of her that had first attracted him to her. In his arms she felt like a bird, delicate and fragile. But it was the rock-solid intelligence and no-nonsense business savvy that had won his respect and his heart. Now the young woman who had opened and was successfully running the largest independent tax service in northeastern Pennsylvania was whimpering like a baby and spouting nonsense about ghosts. He felt distaste and shrugged it away, recognizing it as unworthy and disloyal.

But still—all this drama—it was out of character and he didn't like it, just as he didn't like the real life drama that had been Deidra Shay. To him, Deidra had been too large, too loud, too everything. She didn't fit into his sense of order. As head of the Community Foundation, Brian was what he had to be: calm, self-possessed, charming. His groomed, blond good looks and long, slim body spoke of locker rooms—not as in football but as in golf clubs and squash courts, steam rooms and hot tubs. Just as Jesse's quiet elegance drew him closer, Deidra's screaming opulence had repulsed him.

Jesse's voice interrupted Brian's thoughts. "What about the clothes thrown all over my room? Who do you think did that?" But she knew before he answered.

"Jesse, you were in pretty rough shape last night. Don't you think you could have done it yourself?"

"I think you should believe me." She felt him withdraw, the distance between them leaving her shut out and cold. It crossed her mind that it was a strange thing to notice given the circumstances.

Brian pushed himself away from the table and stood, towering over her. "I'm sorry about Deidra, Jesse, you know I am, but you can't believe you saw her ghost. You really can't believe it stood in the middle of the room and threw things around. I've got to get to work."

"She, not it," Jesse corrected him. Her voice fell to a whisper, "Please." She reached for his hand, held it tight. "Please stay with me—just for a couple of hours?"

Brian's face softened. He lifted her clutching hand to his lips and kissed it gently. "Sorry, Love, but I have a meeting about a possible new endowment. I'll call you later." And like that, he was gone.

CHAPTER 3

Jesse huddled alone in the kitchen crying, sometimes quietly and sometimes in huge gulping sobs that shook her. She could see Deidra slumped against the seat, see her hand trailing on the bus floor, hear herself screaming as she gripped and struggled to hold onto that hand. She felt the long fingers, as cold and unresponsive as ice. She saw the nails, long, polished red-black for the play, looking grotesque on the hand just starting to darken from pooled blood that would never be pumped back to the heart. And she saw a ring. In her memory she felt the ring, hard and cutting, biting into her palm.

Jesse shuddered and thought of Deidra's bottle of whiskey. She could finish it, make her mind a nice smooth blank; her stomach turned over at the thought. She wondered what Brian would think of her slugging

19

down whiskey at ten thirty in the morning—poor Brian, who was mad at her for her unrestrained grief; poophead Brian who made her mad just thinking about him.

She clutched at the fresh anger—anger was so much better than grief. She vented it, wallowed in it, and kicked at the chair he'd been sitting in. It flew across the room, hitting the wall with a satisfying crash.

So, I was dreaming, was I? Well, if you'd stayed the night before, when I begged you to, maybe I wouldn't have needed so much whiskey. If you hadn't run like a coward at the sight of tears, maybe I wouldn't have had that awful dream, you stupid coward!

"I can't roll with this," he had muttered as he left. "You need a good night's sleep." He had patted her head like she was a ranting child who had lost a toy instead of the love of his life who had lost her best friend.

If you had died and Deidra was still alive she would have stayed with me. She hated you and she would have loved me enough to stay anyway, which makes you a perfect shit! Jesse wished she'd been able to scream at him instead of begging.

"Jealous," Jesse spat to the empty room. "He was jealous of Deidra when she was alive and he's jealous of her now that she's dead. He's probably glad!" Jesse threw her full coffee cup into the kitchen sink, splashing its cold dark contents over the kitchen walls. *Stoneware does break after all.*

Something about the smashed chair and shards of glass cleared Jesse's mind. Quiet rushed over her with a sad weariness. *Maybe Brian's right. Maybe I really am out of control.*

Jesse finished cleaning up and dragged herself upstairs to the bathroom. A glimpse in the mirror told her more than she wanted to know about the effect of her rampage. Her face was swollen and blotchy, puffed out of shape by tears and whiskey. She was wearing the same clothes she had put on the day before, and she suddenly realized they smelled of sweat and booze. *Not pleasant*, she thought. A small laugh escaped her. *No wonder Brian ran away.* Brian, who was so meticulous! The fact that he had kissed her seemed amazing now in light of the mirror's reflection.

"But Deidra wouldn't have cared," the anger said.

"Deidra wouldn't have had to sleep with me," the voice of reason replied.

"But she would have," Jesse whispered. "She would have stayed and she would have held me as long as I needed her."

21

With dread, Jesse faced the bedroom. "Every journey begins with a single step," she quoted to herself. That aphorism had gotten her through many a tough spot, and it gave her strength now. Slowly, Jesse pushed the door open to take stock of the mess. She didn't know if she was afraid or hopeful that Deidra was still there.

The hand-painted screen that served as a light filter in front of the window was askew and covered with lacy lingerie that was Jesse's secret obsession. Silk panties, bras and camisoles draped across the top and piled at the bottom. Every piece of underclothing was displayed there in a risqué exhibition. Jesse picked up each delicate piece and folded them neatly back into her top drawer, handling them with just her fingertips, as if even touching them embarrassed her .

Her jeans and skirts, strewn across the floor, were next. She hung them back on the hangers, which had been flung everywhere, including under the bed. As Jesse worked, she tried to imagine herself wreaking so much havoc but couldn't. Even alcohol didn't quite explain this level of frenzy. Oh well, maybe whiskey and grief combined? She just couldn't picture it, but it had to be.

When the last piece of clothing was folded or hung, it dawned on Jesse that the one thing she hadn't found was Deidra's sweater, which she always kept on the hook by the door. It was soft, gray and full of holes. Deidra wouldn't wear it in public, ever, but it was the only thing she wanted to cuddle into when sharing gossip with Jesse. Jesse's room was the only place Deidra didn't feel like she was on display, and she took full advantage of it. Memories flashed through Jesse's mind, of nights and mornings lounging on the deck overlooking the quaint town, drinking whiskey or tea or both as she and Deidra told each other their secrets, sometimes with laughter, often with tears, always with Deidra wrapped in the ancient, worn-out sweater. Memories almost undid her. but Jesse struggled on. There was only the bed to make, and then things would be put to rights.

Jesse pulled her cotton floral print quilt from the bottom of the bed and wondered what would become of Deidra's peach-colored silk throw on the bed in New York. She'd have to remember to get it for Deidra's mother. With guilt, she realized she needed to call Mary and check on how she was handling the loss of her daughter. It was a call she dreaded. How could she comfort Mary when she was so out of control herself?

The bed was a mess—still damp from tears, sweat and what must have been the dregs of her last drink before falling into unconsciousness. She grabbed the pillows and gasped. There, crumpled under the pile of pillows and sheets, was Deidra's sweater. Under the sweater was a diamond ring.

Memory flashed through Jesse, knocking her off of her feet and into the reading chair by the bed. She grasped the ring and cradled it to her chest, seeing again the hand that ring had been on last night. Jesse heard herself screaming, felt herself being pulled away, felt the cut of the ring biting into her palm. Slowly she opened one fist and stared at the deep puncture there. She had taken the ring. Somehow she had taken the ring and now it was here, in her room.

The significance of the diamond struck Jesse like lightning. It was a diamond solitaire—large enough to be significant, but not gaudy—a diamond that had sparkled in the light on the ring finger of Deidra's left hand as her fingers brushed the floor of the train.

That was the news Deidra was so eager to share! That was what the frantic, laughing call from Port Authority had been about. Deidra, her wonderful, dead Deidra, had been engaged.

All the tears Jesse thought she was done crying spilled down her cheeks unchecked. She grabbed the half-empty bottle of whiskey and took a long swig. There she sat, clutching the ring, crying uncontrollably, toasting the unfairness of life and then death—varying the toast with every gulp she took.

CHAPTER 4

Deidra was not having a good day. The only time she could remember a similar experience was when she had tried mushrooms her freshman year in college. Could this be a flashback? It seemed unlikely, given how long it had been since she'd done any tripping, but it felt the same. Time was out of whack. She seemed to be moving from one place to another without any sense of *going* there or *getting* there. She would talk and no one could hear her. Was she really talking at all?

And her body didn't work. She couldn't *feel* anything. She pounded on the door and her hand simply slipped through with no feeling at all. That really was like her tripping days, and she tried to remember if she had taken anything—but no—she never did any kind of drugs during a play run. Had someone slipped her something? It was always a possibility, given the generous and communal spirit of the theatre world. If that was the case, she was going to have a real nasty discussion with someone when things got back to normal.

Normal—now *that* would be good! But nothing was normal. The only thing Deidra could actually feel was the ring, and she clung to it tenaciously. She tried poking herself with a needle but it just went right through her with no pain at all. She did it multiple times until she started to worry about the pain she would be in when this trip, or whatever it was, was over. Maybe she would request another dose the next time she wanted a tattoo or nipple piercing. Now *that* would be nice. But maybe a piercing or tattoo wouldn't take in this condition. She tried sticking the needle into her arm and then letting go, but the needle simply fell right through her and under the bed, where she searched for it but couldn't find it.

It was the noise she hated the most. Voices— crying, laughing, screaming, talking—voices she recognized and voices she couldn't even decipher swarmed around her. She could have sworn she heard her father, but he was dead so that wasn't possible.

His voice, more than any of the others, helped her decide this was, indeed, some hallucination. Maybe 'shrooms laced with LSD? Oh, yeah. Someone was definitely in big trouble when she got back.

And that's what it felt like. Like she was on a journey of some kind, detached from the world she knew and was fond of. A wave of homesickness washed over her. She screamed in heart pain and sorrow.

Jesse must have heard her that time because, even though the bottle of whiskey was empty and Jesse was for all intents and purposes dead to the world, she shuddered when Deidra screamed, and cried out in her sleep.

Jesse's cry was so wrenching that Deidra went to her and took her hand, but Jesse jerked it away, as if the touch was painful, unwanted. Deidra touched Jesse again, and Jesse whimpered. Frustrated, Deidra grabbed Jesse's arm and squeezed, only to see her hand pass right through skin and muscle and go inside Jesse's arm. Curious, Deidra pushed further instead of pulling back, until her arm was inside of Jesse's. She moved her arm up and down, fascinated when Jesse's moved with her.

Now, this was new. Deidra experimented with her new skill, making the unconscious Jesse wave her hand, scratch her head and slap her leg lightly. All this time, Jesse whimpered but didn't wake up. Deidra moved more of herself into Jesse, until her own body was neatly tucked into Jesse's little frame. And what an experiment *that* turned out to be!

Deidra could feel what Jesse felt. She felt cold in Jesse's skin, cold like ice cubes were being rubbed all over her. She could feel the effects of an old-fashioned drunken stupor, could feel the pain in Jesse's neck from falling asleep with her head lolling over the side of the chair—something she was sure Jesse would feel when she woke up. She could feel the rough fabric of the chair, the cool wood of the floor. Thank God! Thank God! She could feel. She laughed with the joy of it, and Jesse whispered her name, "Deidra, Deidra, Deidra."

"Jesse, Jesse, Jesse," Deidra whispered back. She was shocked to hear her own voice coming from Jesse's mouth. In a panic, Deidra withdrew, propelling herself to the furthest corner of the room. How could that be? What kind of hallucination was this, anyway? That was way too freaky. She wouldn't do it again.

Cautiously, Deidra edged back toward Jesse. As she passed the computer, she noticed that it reacted to her. She waved her hand in front of it and crazy lines followed her like one of those balls that follow your finger with lightning-like lines. She touched the keypad, but her fingers glided right through it with no impact at all. Again she waved her hands in the air, and the computer responded. That might be something to try again later if things didn't get back to normal soon.

But she needed things to get back to normal. She had to give Jesse all of the news, including the details of this horrible tripping experience. She had to introduce Jesse to Connor and show her the beautiful diamond ring and make wedding plans and get back to the show. The show! More rehearsals started on Monday, and she had to be in New York. "I need this to fucking stop!" she screamed. "Stop it! Stop it! Stop it!" But whatever was happening didn't stop, and Deidra began to weep in earnest.

Time escaped again. Deidra didn't know how long it had been since Jesse had fallen asleep. The phone had rung off and on for what could have been hours or days, and Jesse slept on. At last, Jesse opened her eyes. Deidra watched with interest as Jesse took a deep shuddering breath and reached for her cell phone on the bedside table.

At first, Jesse's mumbling was unintelligible, but suddenly she sat up straight and something clicked. Her voice grew stronger as she listened intently, only interjecting, "I'm sorry, so sorry," every now and then as the conversation went on. "Yes, I'll be there," Jesse finally said. She wrote what were probably directions or an address on a piece of paper, glanced at the clock and then, as if shocked at the time, jumped to her feet and ran for the bathroom.

Deidra could hear the shower running and thought how nice it would be to take a shower. Maybe she could join Jesse there. If she didn't feel the water, she could just climb inside Jesse for a minute? Just a minute, to feel the water washing over her? Deidra headed for the bedroom door and then stopped. For whatever reason, she couldn't walk through it. It was open. She could hear the water, hear Jesse, but she was locked in the bedroom as surely as if someone had put her in a cage. Frustrated, she lunged at the door but nothing happened.

Another lapse in time. Jesse was back, dressed in a small straight shift. Deidra couldn't help but feel a twinge of envy, even in her altered state. She had never, not once in her life, been able to wear such a thing.

As Jesse grabbed her purse, Deidra felt mounting panic. "Please don't leave me here. Please!"

Just as Deidra was sure she was stuck forever, Jesse turned back, picked up Deidra's ring and slipped it into her pocket. There was a pull so strong it nearly knocked Deidra off her feet as she was propelled forward, through the door and out of the house, down the hill toward South Main Street. Was that it? Was she limited on this crazy journey to only go where Jesse went? Or was it where the ring went? And what was Jesse doing with it, anyway? Possessively, Deidra grabbed the ring and let herself be carried along.

The last place in the world that Deidra thought she would go was to the funeral parlor, but that's where Jesse took her. They were greeted at the door by a tall, thin, soft-spoken man who slipped his arm around Jesse—not in a romantic fashion but in a comforting way—and Deidra was suddenly afraid of what they might be there for. Who had died that meant a great deal to Jesse?

Could it be Brian? If there was anyone Deidra wouldn't mind finding inside the quiet rooms, it was

Brian. As unfair as it was, Deidra felt that Brian brought out the worst in Jesse. All that conservative political crap and the way he never really accepted Deidra herself. But that wasn't fair was it? She certainly wouldn't want something to happen to Connor. But that would explain Jesse's drinking, wouldn't it? And all the hysterical weeping?

Or was it a parent? With Deidra out of commission, Jesse might even get a call if Deidra's own mother had died. But no, there was Mary, looking as haggard and as worn as Jesse, rushing toward them. She threw her entire two-hundred and fifty pounds into Jesse's arms, and they both wept as if the world had ended. Okay, then. Someone they both loved; someone they had in common. But wouldn't that mean it was someone Deidra herself knew and cared about? And why didn't her mother *see* her? Deidra struggled to reach her mother, to slip her own arm around Mary's shoulders. She was shocked when Mary drew back, a startled, frightened look on her face.

"I couldn't call, Mary. I'm so sorry. I just couldn't talk without breaking down completely," Jesse sobbed.

"I need you to help me through this," Mary whispered, tears washing in ignored streaks down her face.

Jesse took Mary in her arms again. "I'm here," she said over and over.

There was another one of those awful time lapses. The three of them were standing in another room. The tall thin man was gently leading Mary toward what looked like a hospital gurney, and then they were looking at a still body covered up to the neck by a lovely handmade quilt.

Deidra and Mary screamed at the exact same moment: Mary as she saw her beloved daughter for the first time since she had received the news; Deidra, as she finally got it.

CHAPTER 5

In the still hours of the night, a sleeping brain can filter out the hustle and bustle of everyday life; disbelief is suspended as the mind opens itself to every imaginable possibility. It was during those dark hours that Jesse struggled out of exhaustion to find a heartbroken Deidra, shaking and in tears, crouched in the corner of her room.

"I'm not ready," she whispered. "No. No. I'm not ready." Jesse watched as Deidra clutched the old gray sweater to her chest and faded—in and out, in and out.

"Oh, Deidra," Jesse said. They cried together through the long, long night.

"Jesse?"

"Hello, Brian."

"I tried to reach you all day yesterday. Are you alright?"

"No, not really."

"I want to come over."

"Please don't."

Long pause. "Have you seen her again?"

"Yes."

"I'm worried about you, Jesse. You shouldn't be alone right now. At least let me take you to dinner. Maybe, with me there, you won't have to keep seeing a ghost."

"That's exactly what I'm afraid of, Brian. I'm not ready to give her up."

Brian knew he had been an ass. He had never experienced the kind of soul-numbing grief Jesse was going through. Even when his own father had died, Brian had been wrapped up in planning the service and overseeing the estate.

It had been Jesse, cool and levelheaded, who had helped him wade through the endless mountain of paper work, determine exactly how much should go to charity, how much be put in trust and what amount and type of annuity to set up for his mother. As a matter of fact, that was when he and Jesse had met.

He smiled to himself, remembering his disbelief and then his gratitude as the improbably small girl with long straight hair quoted inheritance law, chapter and verse, and then explained exactly how to apply it. Without her help he would have been lost, and could have made some very costly mistakes. In retrospect, he realized that Jesse, with her calm reassurance, was the support that had gotten him through the whole ordeal. both financially and emotionally. Now she needed him, and he had walked—no—*run* from the emotional entanglement she presented.

No time like the present, he thought. It was time to stand up and be the support Jesse needed right now. He grabbed his keys and headed out.

While Brian was coming to terms with his behavior toward Jesse, Jesse was busy coming to terms with her responsibility to Deidra and Mary. She made a list of the people she needed to call regarding the funeral service, ordered flowers and reserved hotel rooms. She laid out the clothes she would need and packed an over-night bag so she could stay at the hotel with Deidra's friends after the formal luncheon at the church. She straightened her apartment just in case anyone arrived early and stoically disposed of the empty whiskey bottle, noting that she would need more, possibly a lot more, before this was over. With every completed chore, her anger grew.

Who does he think he is, anyway? What makes him think he can just fix this? Deidra is gone and it isn't right, it isn't fair, it isn't ever going to be okay again! Never! She threw the pillows at the bed. It felt so good she picked them up and threw them again. All the pain of the last two days flooded through her in the form of rage. She found herself cleaning with a ferocity she'd never let take over before. *He left when I begged him to stay, and I don't need him now!* A dark spot appeared in the counter where the thin laminate peeled away while Jesse scrubbed an imaginary stain with a wire brush.

"Look what you made me do!" she screamed at the absent Brian. "Now I have to replace it, you dumb fuck! You moron! You heartless asshole!" She threw the wire brush across the kitchen and slammed her fist against the abused counter. The coffee pot and food processor rattled their disapproval when she shoved them roughly out of the way. The cupboard handles etched scratches down her back as she sunk to the floor. "Oh God, oh God, oh God" she moaned. "I can't stand this. Why didn't he just stay when I asked him to?" She let sobs take over and shake her as she hugged her knees and gave up the idea of doing anything else.

Get a grip, Jesse, she thought. *You're going crazy.* Her shoulders slumped. She took a deep breath and wiped her eyes. *A bath. Just get in some hot water and sit.* And that's what she did.

Deidra watched Jesse's tantrum with a certain amount of satisfaction. *If she dumps Brian because I'm dead it's almost worth it,* she thought maliciously.

Deidra had discovered she could leave the ring. She couldn't go far, but she could go, and that made life a lot more interesting. *Life*, she thought and laughed—an angry guttural laugh that would have frightened Jesse if she could have heard it. *Makes life more interesting,* Deidra repeated to herself as she danced around the bedroom, chuckling at her own sense of humor. She could move things. It was a matter of *focusing.* She practiced, first with the gauzy curtains hanging over Jesse's bed, then with bigger heavier things, rearranging the pastel bottles on Jesse's dresser, opening and closing the bedroom door and finally moving the reading chair ever so little.

It was Deidra who heard Brian's car pull into the driveway, Deidra who went downstairs and saw the kitchen door knob turn as Brian used the key Jesse had given him. While Jesse let hot bathwater pour over her aching head and sank lower into the bubbles, it was Deidra who held the doorknob and didn't let him in.

CHAPTER 6

Connor hadn't slept since Mary's hysterical phone call the morning Deidra died. He hadn't done a lot of things, like shower or eat or get sober. Who wanted to be sober? How could anyone stand to be sober knowing that Deidra was gone and not coming back?

There were things to do, of course: contact the theatre, plan on attending the god-awful funeral in that god-awful town somewhere in the boonies, pile Deidra's clothes on his bed and bury himself in them just to smell her before the perfume was gone. There were things to do—the first two took ten minutes—the last one took every second of every twenty-four hour period since then. He had changed his mind; there was a hell and he was living in it.

Connor stared at the suitcase, trying to remember exactly when he had packed it. Well, he had done it and that was a good thing. He might have missed the funeral altogether if Bethany hadn't called to offer him a ride. "You don't want to be on a stinky, crowded bus, do you? I'm driving and have lots of room." Her tone was a little *too* friendly. He wasn't sure how he knew but he did. It set his teeth on edge. Bethany had never been subtle.

And he did want to be on a stinky crowded bus. He wanted to see everything that Deidra had seen in those last couple of hours before she died. In his fantasies, he found the person who had fired that shot and took revenge. The form of revenge changed every time because he couldn't't' think of anything bad enough, painful enough to equal what he was going through now.

"You really do have to get from Scranton to Montrose," Bethany had insisted. "It's another hour from the bus stop. At least let me pick you up for that."

"They have taxis, don't they?"

"I .... I'm honestly not sure. I don't think so." Bethany sounded sincere about that. Her hesitation was enough to make Connor call around until he found a limo company with a driver willing to get him to and from Montrose and any place else he needed to be in the next few days. Thank god for money—it did have its benefits.

With half an hour to go until the limo arrived. Connor found himself sitting in a daze in front of his computer. Kill time, kill himself—it was a toss-up. *I don't mean that, do I?* It was a little scary how hard it was to decide on the answer. *Get me through this, Deidra.* He recognized it as a prayer. She was his goddess, and it was perfectly normal to pray to her, wasn't it?

He thought about the hours they had spent on Facebook. They had posted pictures so Mary could keep up with Deidra's busy life. Deidra had shown him Jesse's posts because she wanted him to "love her as much as I do."

"You left me to see her and it killed you. I hate her, okay? And that's the way it is. Selfish bitch—her, not you. Sorry Dee." He dropped the menu and opened Facebook. He wanted to see Deidra smiling into the camera for her profile picture. She had wanted to post the two of them together but he had refused. "Don't ruin the picture," he'd told her. She had laughed, he had snapped her picture with the camera in his cell phone and that was the picture he wanted to see now.

He opened the site and stared. It took a moment to realize what he was seeing; even then it didn't make sense. His roar of rage woke up the neighbors and sent pigeons flapping madly off the roof. He opened up his cell to the number Deidra had given him before she got on the bus and punched the call button.

The morning of Deidra's funeral dawned dark and gray. Wind pelted cold rain through Jesse's open window, knocked over the lightweight screen and sprayed icy droplets across her face. She lay shivering in the in the damp bed, dreading the day, putting off facing it.

Deidra hadn't made an appearance, and her absence had kept Jesse awake as much as her presence had during the nights before. *Where is she? Somewhere else? With someone else?* A pang of jealousy surprised Jesse. *I have to be the only person in the world who actually wants to be haunted.*

When her phone rang, Jesse glanced at the clock, surprised anyone would call so early. Had she overslept? No. The clock was set for six AM and the alarm hadn't gone off unless she had slept right through. But no. The hands read four-thirty. Jesse grabbed her cell.

"Hello?" Bad news. It had to be.

"What the fuck do you think you're doing?" A male voice screamed at her, freezing her insides.

"Who is this?" Jesse heard her own voice squeak and fought to bring it under control. "Who are you and what do you want?"

"You know what I'm talking about! This isn't fucking cool, you bitch!"

"Listen … you have a wrong number. I'm sorry for whatever happened, but you obviously have the wrong number. I'm hanging up."

Immediately her phone rang again. Jesse took a deep breath and hit the answer button.

"Don't hang up on me," the male voice growled. "Deidra loved three people—you, me and Mary, and Mary doesn't even know *how* to use Facebook! She sure as hell wouldn't have Deidra's password. You fucking pull a stunt like that again and I swear I'll press charges for … I don't know … impersonating a *dead* person?"

"I have no idea what you're talking about!" Jesse screamed back. "And I don't know if there is any law like you're talking about, but there *is* a law against harassment. Whoever you are, you will not call me again!" Jesse hit the disconnect button and waited, shivering in the dark. A lunatic. Some mean, demented lunatic. How the hell had he gotten her number?

The phone rang a third time. Jesse sat on the bed, her knees pulled to her chest and let it go to voice mail. "Jesse?" the deep voice growled. "Jesse, I know you can hear me. Pick up the goddamn phone!"

But Jesse didn't pick up the phone, and she sure as hell wasn't going back to sleep. Whoever that was, he knew her name. He knew Deidra and Mary. What was it he had said? Something about Facebook? Jesse scrambled out of the covers and felt her way through the half-light to her computer. She hit the on button and waited for what seemed like minutes for Facebook to come up and another minute for her brain to register what she was seeing.

Facebook asked, "What's on your mind?"

Deidra posted, "Boo!"

Jesse felt the air leave her stomach, her lungs, her head in one instantaneous rush. For the first time in her life she fainted.

Jesse's scrambled brain woke up and immediately searched for the clock: four-forty-five.

Okay, a phone call, turning on the computer, seeing the post, passing out; it hadn't taken much time. She found "Calls Received" on her phone and hit call on the unknown number.

"Yeah," the graveled low voice answered.

"It wasn't me," Jesse said in her most professional and reasonable voice, "but you said Deidra loved me, Mary and you. That makes you the fiancé, right? I suggest you sober up before the service. Oh yes, and I don't know where you found my number, but I would deeply appreciate it if you would lose it." Before there could be a response Jesse hit disconnect.

The Brookdale Cemetery was small but old. Ancient tombstones from pre-Civil War days leaned awkwardly among trees, weather-beaten and tired. Myrtle covered the shaded areas, already showing purple flowers even in what was early spring in northeastern Pennsylvania. Jesse wondered how Deidra felt about being buried so far from the city and the constant nightlife she loved so much. Worse, Liberty Township was dry—no bars allowed. Jesse made a note to herself to deliver an occasional bottle of whiskey for Deidra here on this cold, lonely hill.

Deidra had touched a variety of lives. Jesse stood near the gravesite and categorized them. There were the church folks clustered around Mary; where the hell had they gotten those clothes? Vintage 1960? Polyester suits, for God's sake! Oh my God—light blue, tan, pink—and was that really an Easter bonnet from God knows when? And Mary herself, dressed in black—but definitely not a Jones of New York—black pumps with overlying rolls accentuating her swollen ankles. A black pillbox hat perched on the permed gray hair, effectively augmenting Mary's badly swollen eyes and deeply lined cheeks. Jesse's heart nearly broke for her. Poor Mary.

And there was the New York crowd, playing their part. There was a certain beauty about the uniform black and white; women, emaciated and stark wearing black sheaths, even in the bitter cold. High heels sank into mud, and-broad brimmed hats shaded the kohl-darkened eyes of New York's up-and-coming hopefuls. The men, dressed in black suits with long overcoats, graciously removed those same coats and draped them around the slim shoulders of their female counterparts, sacrificing Evan Picone, Versace and Donna Karan to the inclement weather.

There were the outsiders—people who came on behalf of the true grievers, lending support, or those with their own one-man connections. Brian was there, standing elegant and erect in dark gray, not black, looking out of place and uncomfortable but determined. He moved toward Jesse but she averted her eyes, stopping him as effectively as if she had screamed, "No!" which was what she was thinking.

Jesse stepped closer to her small group of college friends who had been there in the beginning with Deidra and herself. It was hard to believe that the eclectic group of drug-experimenting-alcohol-abusing-class-skipping members of their class had turned into this professional, well-behaved community, but they had, and Jesse joined them, soaking up the comfort they provided. Stan reached out and took her hand; she squeezed his in appreciation.

There were people Jesse didn't know, of course, in clusters and alone, all gathered to say goodbye to a woman they would never be able to replace. Jesse searched their faces trying to find the one person who might have called her in the wee hours of the morning. She briefly studied a man who kept himself apart and ruled him out based solely on the fact that he didn't fit anywhere and Deidra had been firmly ensconced with the theatre group when she got engaged. The man was huge—six foot three? Six foot four? He was inappropriately dressed in chinos and a plaid shirt, with a corduroy jacket that had seen better days. The unseasonable May weather had flattened his shaggy red hair and shaggier beard until they appeared to be dirty, hugging his head in an unkempt mop. Jesse placed him in the "former lover" category, possibly a lumberjack or construction worker who knew Deidra from the old days before college, before New York.

She surveyed the theatre group closely. These were the people Deidra had been closest to, and one of those indecipherable replicas had to be the man she had agreed to marry. Jesse couldn't find anyone who appeared unique enough to warrant consideration.

And there were crows—a ridiculous number of them, congregating quietly on the trees and electrical wires, lining the narrow dirt road to the cemetery. A shudder went up Jesse's spine. Hadn't she read something about crows and the spirits of the dead? It was eerie.

The young minister from the Free Methodist church that Mary attended stepped to the head of the gravesite and spoke softly. "We are here today to say our final farewells to our sister-in-Christ, Deidra Shay. Deidra is with her Lord in heaven today, and while our hearts are broken we know the angels are rejoicing."

Jesse shifted uncomfortably. *She had her own faith—not your bigoted, small-minded nonsense,* Jesse wanted to say, but this service was for the living, wasn't it? And certainly Mary needed to hear that her daughter had died a Christian.

"Lo, though I walk through the valley of death, I will fear no evil," the minister continued. Jesse blocked him out.

Deidra was terrified. What would happen when this was over, when they threw roses and dirt on her casket and put it into the ground? Would she just swoop into that God-awful box and stop? Stop seeing, stop thinking, stop *being*? She clung to the ring lying quietly in Deidra's pocket and waited. She hated the dark—always had. What if she didn't stop being but was locked forever underground with no air and no light? *No! No! No! Don't do this!* But the minister just kept going, totally unaware that he was moving Deidra toward a hell on Earth that made her sick with fear.

Mom! I'm here. Can't you see me? Can't you hear me? Connor? Please, please, please make him stop! Why can't anyone hear me? Aren't ghosts supposed to be felt or something? Frantically, Deidra went to the people who loved her best. The only response she got when she touched them was that awful shudder as they felt the icy cold she seemed to generate. *Jesse, save me!*

"Let us pray," said the minister. Deidra squeezed her eyes shut and clamped her hands over her ears. She couldn't, just couldn't, listen or watch as the minister lead them in "The Lord's Prayer.

"Come with us," said the crows, and Deidra found herself being lifted into the air, borne away on hundreds of wings

Surrounded by her circle of friends, Jesse let herself go. Tears rolled down her cheeks, dripped off of her chin and wet the neck of her dress. She wondered if Deidra would ever visit her again or if this was really and truly the end. They stood hip to hip, she and the other college friends, dreading the end of this service that had brought them together. Just as the minister invited everyone to bow their heads one last time, a roar of wings and cawing filled the air. The crows rose simultaneously and circled the gathering on the ground. They flew higher and higher until they were small specks in the sky, their voices eerily calling from further and further away.

Jesse buried her head in Stan's shoulder and wept. Brian watched the guy he didn't know put his arms around Jesse and hold her tight and wished with all of his heart that he was the one giving comfort. Connor, alone and wanting it that way, stared stonily ahead and wondered how the hell he was supposed to go on living when all of this was over.

Deidra was exhilarated. Flying with the crows was the greatest freedom she had ever known. She could see her family and friends in a circle around her grave and laughed. Somehow she knew that she wasn't going to be joining her body inside the awful coffin which would be sealed inside the even-worse waterproof, airproof vault.

"The worms crawl in, the worms crawl out," she sang loudly and laughed at the wonder of her own humor.

"What were you so worried about?" The female voice of the crow was a gentle, reassuring one.

"I never died before," Deidra quipped back. "It isn't all that easy."

"Oh—that!" the crow laughed. "You know, death has very little to do with living—unless you want it to."

Then Deidra was falling, not in a scary rush, but floating, right back to Jesse and the comfort of the ring.

CHAPTER 7

The reception following the funeral was held in the basement of the Free Methodist church. All of Mary's friends had pitched in to provide lasagna made with over-cooked noodles, cottage cheese, canned sauce, hamburger and American cheese slices. "As good as any Italian restaurant (she said it *eye*-talian), don't you think?" Mary commented to any and all who could hear her. Jesse tried not to wince as she nodded agreeably. The New York actors simply looked the other way as if it were more than they could stand.

There was tons of food, including the necessary green Jell-O-salad, baked beans, tuna and egg-salad finger sandwiches cut into little triangles with the crust removed from super-soft bread, both macaroni and potato salads and various cakes and cookies. Someone had had the good sense to provide a tray of fresh fruit and vegetables, which Jesse found tucked into a corner behind the Ritz crackers and "cheddar" cheese. She gratefully put some on the brightly flowered paper plate and stood chewing celery sticks while waiting for time to pass. She sipped some pink fruit punch and wished desperately for a shot of rum to put in it.

As soon as possible, she and her friends had plans to meet at the hotel and grieve in their own way. The New Yorkers had been invited. Jesse had to stay at the church as long as Mary wanted her there, but many of Deidra's other friends had already left. Jesse again noticed the red-headed man in the worn jacket. He was staying close to Mary, slipping a protective arm around her when her lips quivered during yet another story about Deidra's childhood. A family member, then? Maybe. Jesse unintentionally made eye contact briefly and was shocked at the pain and fury there. Someone who had been close to Deidra, then; someone who wasn't handling her death very well.

Jesse's head pounded. The pain had started days ago and was nearly blinding. She was relieved when Mary's group of church ladies whispered that they thought they should take Mary home. Jesse kissed Mary's cheek and folded the plump body into her arms. "Call if you need me," Jesse said softly. "I'll come, any day, any time." Mary simply nodded, fresh tears washing down her face.

As Jesse turned to leave Mary grabbed her arm. "Jesse, I don't think you've met Deidra's fiancé, Connor O'Dea. Connor, this is Jesse Garner. Jesse, this is Connor."

Jesse felt her head pound even harder. This slovenly giant was the love of Deidra's life? "I believe we've spoken, Jessica," he said as he shook her hand. She recognized the voice from the wee hours of morning and jerked away from him.

"Jesse," she corrected him. "I'm sorry for your loss." The cold tone of her voice alerted Mary to the tension between them and she looked back and forth, back and forth, with her soft, startled eyes.

"You know each other?" Mary asked in surprise. "But I've only met Connor a few times and I thought Deidra said …" Her voice drifted off in painful confusion. "I mean, Deidra was so excited that the two of you would finally meet."

"We spoke briefly on the phone this morning," Jesse assured her with a fake smile. There was no reason to upset Mary with all she was going through.

"I'll see you at the hotel," Connor said, "Your friends invited me to join them."

"Consider yourself uninvited," Jesse muttered under her breath and was surprised to see a smile start at the corner of his mouth.

"I'll just see Mary home and then join you there. I'm eager to meet Deidra's college friends. You all seem to have such great imaginations." At the undercurrent of threat in his voice, Jesse gritted her teeth.

"I'm just afraid you'll feel out of place," she replied, barely able to keep her own malice from coming through.

Mary smiled and gushed, "Oh, I'm sure Deidra would want Connor to meet all of you." She gazed up at the big man with a look Jesse was shocked to recognize as adoration—or was it flirtation? "He's been so, so good to me—such a comfort." Mary took Connor's arm, her eye lashes actually batting as she gazed lovingly up at him.

Jesse relented. "Just get there before we fall asleep," she said sweetly. "You wouldn't want to wake anyone up." Her blue eyes met his dark brown ones. She was gratified to see him flush, but whether from anger or embarrassment she couldn't tell.

"No," he said. "I wouldn't want to do anything like that unless it couldn't be avoided."

Jesse hoped she looked haughty and dismissive as she walked quickly away, but she doubted it. She was afraid she looked exactly like she felt—like a mouse scampering for its hole.

They had chosen the hotel for one reason: the Holiday Inn Express was the only real hotel around. As Jesse stepped into the sparkling clean lobby, she couldn't help but wonder what Deidra's friends thought of a rural area with only one place to stay. All of them, with the exception of Jesse herself, had graduated and found success in the arts in New York, Boston and Philadelphia. Jesse had dropped out and returned later to study accounting, her days as a photographer buried in the necessity to earn a living in some practical field in a town where no one, absolutely no one, earned their living just painting, acting or writing.

A light scent of chlorine near the elevator told Jesse there was a pool nearby. For a moment she felt the urge to find it, remove all of her clothes and immerse herself in it; forget everyone else and just soak for an hour or a day or however long it took to wash the past week away. Jesse winced as she recognized the fantasy of floating naked in the hotel pool as something she and Deidra might actually have done in those college years before real life had jumped in. Deidra, of course, would still do it without hesitation but Jesse—well, those days were long gone. With a little shock Jesse realized she missed them terribly.

"Jesse." Jesse jumped when Brian touched her arm.

"What are you doing here?" Jesse was surprised at the venom in her own voice and softened it. "I'm sorry, Brian. But what are you doing here? You aren't invited."

Brian let his hand drop and stepped back. That distance again—Jesse could feel him detaching himself from her and for a moment she wanted to reach out and fix it.

"I thought you might need me and I wanted to be here for you," he said. "I guess I was mistaken."

"These are Deidra's friends, Brian. We loved her. You didn't like her and you don't belong here."

"Deidra and I both love you, Jesse. I thought … I guess I thought I could make this easier." The silence between them grew. How long? Seconds, surely, but it felt like minutes.

When Jesse did speak, she didn't look at Brian but rather kept her eyes on the floor and spoke so softly he had to lean forward slightly to hear her. "When I first went to college I didn't want to be there. I was frightened and out of place. All those kids—sure of themselves—already grouped together like they'd been friends forever. I was lost and Deidra found me. She found all of us and gave us a place to belong. She babysat us through our growing years, provided an apartment where we could feel safe. Sal was so shy he couldn't answer questions in class; Jake got drunk every night and sat around in his underwear; Suzanne was gay when being gay wasn't acceptable; and Paul—Paul didn't even know if he was straight or gay and was trying everything. Deidra herself was hunched and overweight, uncomfortable with her height. She was very Goth back then—black hair, black nails, black lipstick. But she was warm and accepting. We were misfits and Deidra loved every one of us and we loved her back the way only lost artists can love."

Jesse's voice grew stronger. When she did meet Brian's eyes, her own were filled with defiance. "I've slept with half the men in that room, Brian. I've done things you wouldn't guess in a million years and I never told you because I knew you wouldn't love that

Jesse. God knows, I didn't even love her, but Deidra did. She, along with my friends on the third floor, walked me through bad trips, held my head while I threw up after drinking the night away, covered for me when I stopped going to classes and basically watched me fuck up my life and loved me anyway. And you know what? They love me now, too, as straight and narrow and correct as I've become."

A harsh laugh escaped Jesse's lips. A laugh so out of character that Brian could only stare in shock at this person he had never seen before. "I didn't own all those lovely silky underwear you like so much. God! I hardly ever wore underwear! That would have meant doing laundry, and who could be bothered with all of that?"

Jesse's laughter turned into sobs and she stood straighter, defying him. As she raised her voice, the front desk clerk glanced nervously their way and then busied himself with the computer. Jesse didn't care. "I'm the only person out of that group that didn't follow my art. I don't even own a camera. I haven't painted a picture in ten years, and you know what? I'm not even the same person anymore, and I don't want to be. But part of me misses that wild child. Part of me wonders where all the passion and no-holds-barred attitude went. I miss her. Deidra kept her alive for me, and now Deidra is dead, and that person died with her. And I miss her! I'm going up there to join my friends and grieve for the one who brought us together and got us through, and the last thing I need in the room is some watchdog who doesn't know what the hell we're even talking about. Go away, Brian. You've never been lost in your entire life."

"So you're going up there to relive your college days? Maybe have an orgy or two?" Brian's bitterness crept out of him before he even knew it was coming. "Is that why I can't be with you? Because you want to reenact being eighteen? And I've never been lost? How would you know? I was lost until I found you!" Brian grabbed Jesse to him roughly. She was too shocked to react but when she did she pushed him hard enough to make him stumble backward, barely catching himself against the wall. Jesse noticed the desk clerk watching them again, his hand posed near the phone. She lowered her voice. She wondered how long it would take for the police to arrive if he did make a call.

"I told you I'm not that person anymore! But I was that person and up there, with people who knew me, I don't have to pretend. I don't have to be afraid of saying something inappropriate or behaving in a way I'll regret. I don't have to be careful! I'm always so god-damned careful! I knew you wouldn't understand. You can't understand. Now leave me alone!"

Jesse hit the elevator button so hard her fingernail broke. She instinctively stuck the finger in her mouth, and Brian was struck by how small she looked, how young. Regret flooded over him. "Jesse, I'm sorry. I didn't mean it. Please ..." But the elevator door opened and closed and Jesse was gone, leaving Brian in a whirl of emotions he couldn't sort out.

CHAPTER 8

The college friends had taken the entire third floor of the Holiday Inn. By unlocking the connecting doors, they had created a meeting area large enough to accommodate all of them and still have room for small groups or individuals to get some privacy when grief became overwhelming.

Deidra's threatre troupe had been invited, and they stood together, quietly conversing. Jesse's friends were more spread out, already shed of shoes and ties and jackets. Bottles of Jack Daniels sat on tables along with shot glasses. Tonight every drink would be a tribute to Deidra. Someone handed Jesse a shot, and she carried it carefully, aware that she was already too volatile to trust herself. The conversation with Brian had brought up old memories, and, no matter what she had said, she had no intention of reverting to her younger self.

The sweet smoke of a joint being passed on an outside balcony struck her, making her stomach turn. She had never liked that smell and apparently still didn't. Part of her was surprised that this group of highly successful professionals still got stoned. She had a fleeting image of being hauled off to jail for illegal substances, her accounting career flushed forever down the drain, and flinched. People didn't trust accountants who did drugs, but then maybe actors, writers, graphic artists and film producers lived by different standards.

Here and there, laptops ran slideshows of Deidra as a child, Deidra in college and Deidra in various roles she had played on stage. Actors watched in interest, seeing a Deidra before she was the glamorous New Yorker, and the college crowd watched in appreciation of who Deidra had become, sharing memories of shows they had gone to see. Paul offered to upload clips from a pilot Deidra had volunteered to be in during his college days—before anyone was anyone— and then admitted with a laugh that it might be a little more than they wanted to see; it had been a not-so-soft-porn flick.

Sal moved to Jesse's side and handed her a lit cigarette, which she accepted gratefully, forgetting she hadn't smoked in years. He stayed beside her, his arm protectively around her waist. Jesse noticed his wife wasn't present. No spouses were present, actually. This was just them—the people who had known Deidra and loved her. She was grateful not to have to shake hands and omit any reference to pasts that might make home-life difficult when the party was over. With a pang she remembered the things she had told Brian and wondered if she'd ever see him again. Probably not. The sorrow that flashed through her heart at the thought surprised her. She made herself focus on people in the room.

A stunning man walked toward Jesse and suddenly Jesse burst into happy laughter. "My God, Suzanne! You're the best looking man in the room!"

"Don't flatter me too much, you old tease. We both know you aren't interested," Suzanne quipped and hugged Jesse. "You look great."

"And you," Jesse returned the hug with real affection. Suzanne had kissed Jesse once, and once had been enough to verify Jesse's firm heterosexual status.

"I understand Connor is invited to join us," Suzanne whispered. "I also hear he's a real Neanderthal. Have you met him?"

"Don't insult the Neanderthals," Jesse whispered back. As if on cue, the room fell silent and everyone turned. Connor filled the doorway, his red hair bushed out, the old jacket standing out like a sore thumb next to the expensive tasteful clothing in front of him.

"Holy fuckin' shit," Suzanne gasped. "That isn't him, is it?"

"The fiancé himself," Jesse assured her, and stepped behind Sal to keep from being seen. "He doesn't like me very much."

The New Yorkers gathered around Connor, murmuring sympathies and taking turns hugging him. Paul stepped forward to put the requisite shot of whiskey in Connor's hand. "To Deidra," Paul said, and raised his own glass. Connor downed the whiskey and held out the shot glass for another which Paul quickly provided.

Everyone grabbed glasses as Connor raised his to all of them. "To Deidra," he repeated, and everyone joined him in his second drink. Obediently, Jesse downed the shot she had been holding and felt it burn her already abused stomach. The last two days of drinking at home had left her raw.

"Deidra loved you, man, so we love you, too," Paul said. "Welcome." A third shot followed. Jesse felt her head start to swim. She vaguely remembered that she hadn't eaten anything but celery as she sank into a chair. It wouldn't do to draw attention to herself by falling down.

A startled gasp, followed by, "Oh my God!" drew everyone's attention. One of the theatre group stood in front of a computer, pointing at the screen. Her eyes were wide and staring, her mouth frozen open. "I was just looking ..." she stammered, "I mean, I was just wondering what Deidra had last posted, and then ... and Connor ... we were doing shots ..." Her voice dropped off as she burst into tears and buried her head on the closest shoulder.

They gathered around the computer to stare, mesmerized by the screen. Ten seconds ago Deidra had posted one word. "Cheers," she said.

There were little screams, gasps, angry murmurs and Connor roaring, "What sick fuck did that!" Jesse ran to the closest bathroom and threw up into the toilet bowl, her mind recording from a distance that whiskey burns as much coming up as it does going down. She leaned her head gratefully against the cold porcelain, turning slightly at a sound behind her.

Connor stood in the bathroom door, a scowl screwing his face into a terrifying mask. "Fuck you," Jesse said weakly, and turned her face away.

CHAPTER 9

Deidra was having a blast. She rode the ring in Jesse's pocket to the reception at the church, where every whisper of her name made her stronger. She wanted to comfort her mother but held back, not sure if the fragile Mary could stand the strain. Still, all those nice things being said, all those stories being retold drew her from group to group. She could see the whole room, feel every emotion and in her ears the call of "Deidra, Deidra, Deidra," filled her with elation.

But the church had been nothing compared to the upstairs rooms at the Holiday Inn. This was definitely the best party she'd ever thrown. Who knew dying could be so liberating? She was called, time after time, by every person in the room. They gave her

71

strength—she could feel it. Boldly she touched them, here and there, each time drawing a little of their energy.

Her thoughts were disjointed, and that funny time-lapse thing still happened, but here, where her name and thoughts of her were in every head and heart, she could maintain being more than at any other time since dying.

She flitted in and out of Jesse so she could actually feel those hugs. Impatiently, she waited for Jesse to join in shots to see if she could feel that, too— the rush of whiskey. She wanted to taste it again, get a little buzz. But Jesse wasn't cooperating. Jesse was too lost in emotions to even feel Deidra zooming in and out. That was okay. It would be a long night, and sooner or later Jesse was bound to let her guard down. She always did.

Meanwhile, Deidra went from picture to picture and hung out by the computers. She played with the electronic response to her presence, waiting for someone to notice the effect she had on the screen, but there was too much going on. Deidra wanted to be noticed. She wanted to join in the fun, and being noticed was something she had come to love throughout her years on stage.

The stronger Deidra got, the bolder she became. She couldn't talk to Sal, but she could trigger his brain to remember. She reminded him of the night they had gone moon-dancing, showing him images of her naked body so vivid he got an erection and had to step away from Jesse to compose himself. Deidra laughed.

She ran a finger up Suzanne's spine, knowing from her experiences with Jesse that her touch was cold, cold, cold. Suzanne shivered and looked around for the cause while Deidra drew away. For a second, she felt like Suzanne would see her if she stayed too close, and who knew? Maybe she would.

A little experimenting and Deidra realized she could stand next to someone or dance around a group and watch her friends turn expectantly only to become puzzled when no one was there. She moved a chair the slightest bit in the oldest prank in the world and saw Jim catch Kathy just before she missed her seat and fell to the floor. Every time she touched someone, they drew away a little, with a shiver and glance at the air conditioning vent as if suspecting something had gone wrong with the system.

She inhaled the smoke from the balcony, hoping for a free hit of grass, but it didn't work. She would have to be inside someone to get high, she decided, but slipping into anyone but Jesse felt uncomfortable. She felt impatient with Jesse again, wondering if Jesse would do anything that would give Deidra a little more of a physical experience but, other than having a cigarette, Jesse didn't seem inclined to party.

Then Connor arrived—her big, beautiful man, standing like a mountain among all those little hills. Connor had come and brought opportunity with him. His single focus on his love and grief for Deidra pulled at her until she almost felt whole. Power flooded into her, magnified her. Jesse did three shots of whiskey, one after the other, and Deidra was right—she could slip inside Jesse and get a buzz. Fun!

More than anything else, though, Deidra wanted to let Connor know she was there, really there. When Sandra pulled up Facebook, Deidra saw her moment and grabbed it. Just before the third shot in honor of her memory she posted, "Cheers!" and all hell broke loose. Jesse ran to throw up, making Deidra grateful that she had exited Jesse's body before it happened. If there was anything Deidra hated it was throwing up.

When Jesse turned away from Connor, she closed her eyes and waited for a repeat of the early morning accusations. Instead, she felt a cold cloth being gently dabbed on the back of her neck and the inside of her wrists. Softly, ever so softly, warm hands turned her head and applied another cloth to her mouth, her face.

"It's okay," a lovely baritone voice murmured. "It's okay." She was lifted from the floor and carried to a bed, where she buried her head in a pillow and cried. She wasn't sure how long she laid there, but through it all the same warm hands stroked her hair; the same soft voice assured her it would be alright. It was the first time since Deidra's death that anyone had cried with her, and the relief was nearly shattering. She had comforted Mary, had raged in her own despair and had begged Brian to understand, but this was different. This man shared her grief and understood it. He stayed until she was drained of emotion.

When she was finally quiet Connor helped Jesse sit up. "Thank you," she said. "It's all been too much. Too much." She would have started crying again if it hadn't been for his smile. It was so genuine, so understanding that she smiled back and gave in to the sudden urge to throw her arms around him and laugh. "Who would have thought that you'd be the one to make me feel better? Thank you, Connor."

He hugged her back. "I guess you're not a fuckin' bitch after all." Their laughter carried healing relief.

Connor gave Jesse his hand and helped her stand and straighten her clothes. When they walked back into the room, concerned friends glanced at them nervously and then turned away as if something else had caught their attention. Connor smiled as he addressed the room, "You can look now. We're doing much better."

Soft laughter greeted his announcement. Friends gathered around them for a group hug, talking over each other. Who had posted on Deidra's wall? Who would do that? Was it really Deidra? Jesse felt reality shift again and grasped Connor's hand. He held on to her, keeping her steady.

Gradually, people slipped away in conversation, two and three at a time, until Connor and Jesse were left alone. He took her by the shoulders, guided her to a couch and disappeared for a moment, only to return with a tall glass filled with something purple. "Lots of ginger ale and a little blackberry brandy," he explained. "Sip, don't drink. It'll help your stomach."

"And what are you having?"

"Nothing wrong with my stomach," he grinned, and poured half of a glass of brandy for himself. "She loved you like crazy," Connor said softly. "I heard so much about you it made me jealous sometimes."

"She agreed to marry you without even telling me," Jesse replied. "Deidra always talked to me about her big decisions; then she was on that bus wearing a diamond, and I didn't even know you existed. It took a day for me to realize that it was an engagement ring." Jesse slipped the ring out of her pocket, tentatively holding it out to Connor. "This is yours," she said. "I couldn't let them bury it with her."

He stared at the ring, started to take it and then drew back. "I don't think I can bear the pain," he said. "Please, could you keep it for now?"

Jesse nodded her head and slipped it back into her pocket. She didn't know if she was relieved or reluctant to keep it. There was something unnerving about the ring. It had become an obsession that she wasn't comfortable with, but was powerless to change. "Just for now, but it's yours." Connor nodded.

"So, tell me how you met our Deidra," Jesse suggested. "I'll tell you mine if you tell me yours." She waggled her eyebrows in exaggerated suggestion that was so unlikely and so ridiculous that Connor burst into laughter.

"Okay, so where do I start? I was at NYU making a film on the up-and-coming-hopefuls and their self-imposed quest for acting careers when someone suggested I talk to Deidra Shay. The first time I saw her, she blew my mind. That was it for me."

"What was your first impression?" Jesse prodded. Their focus brought Deidra to the couch, and she settled behind, beside, around them as they talked. Quietly, other people drifted closer, wanting to allow Jesse and Connor their privacy but also wanting to hear these two, Deidra's closest and dearest, recount her life from their views.

"She was gloriously flamboyant," Connor mused, his eyes softening as he looked back to another time and place. "She strutted into the room I used for taping interviews in this ridiculous lacy black slip-dress and high boots—all six foot of her. She had this low, throaty voice and when she reached out to shake my hand I nearly jumped from the electricity she generated."

"And that was it? It was mutual?"

"Not quite. She started off with that wild suggestive stuff but when I asked her what made her start acting she got serious and quiet. She said it was you, Jesse. She said you made her go on her first audition."

"It was all of us," Jesse pointed around the room to indicate the college friends. "She was nervous so we all went with her and waited outside. I thought she was going to chicken out but she didn't, and then she got the lead role."

"Anyway," Connor continued, "I was ready for a wild night with this woman who oozed sex; what I got was a long walk in Central Park while she told me what it was like to be the Hulk in a world full of petite girls with mini-skirts and perky breasts." He paused and raised his eyebrows. "She said you bought her a push-up bra."

"I did," Jesse confirmed with a giggle. "I'd seen her naked."

"We all had," Sal interjected. "She didn't see any reason to leave the room or close the door when she was changing." His smile was fond rather than lascivious. "It was a revelation to us poor geek boys. Most of us hadn't even seen our sisters' panties, and here was this woman-child walking around buck naked." A chorus of laughter followed, along with nodded agreements.

"Anyway, Deidra always wore these long black sacks, and no one knew that she had this knock-dead body, so I took her to a store and had her fitted for a push-up bra as a birthday present. My God! You should have seen the change! Guys started falling over themselves just to look at her."

"We bought her the rest, too," Paul interjected. "Low-cut black top and form fitting jeans. We couldn't have her auditioning looking like a bad Halloween costume."

"I want to thank you, one and all." Connor saluted the room with his glass. "I'm not sure Goth garb would have caught my attention in quite the same way." His tone changed, becoming soft with memory. "Anyway, she went from 'keep up with me if you dare,' to 'be gentle, please, don't hurt me,' and it blew me away."

"Were you? Gentle, I mean?" Jesse was curious. She knew both sides of Deidra and wasn't sure which man Deidra would have fallen in love with.

"I was whatever she wanted me to be at any given time," Connor said, looking straight at Jesse.

"She played roles and I was always ready to be her leading man, good or bad. Mostly, I respected her work and the almost puritan work ethic she lived by. Did you know she never had sex with anyone connected with a play? She said that when she was successful she didn't want anyone saying she had slept her way to the top."

Jesse nodded. That was the Deidra she knew—devil and angel all the way—self-conscious and still shockingly confident. It didn't surprise her that Deidra had fallen in love with a man who could match her on both levels.

"I'm kind of a workaholic myself," Connor continued. "I understood her and she understood me. She was honest and loyal to a fault. And joyous. I've never known anyone else who reveled in life like she did. How could I not love her? She was contagious."

"And generous," Jesse added. "She gave herself one-hundred percent to her friends. I don't know where I'd be without her. Dead, maybe. She got me through …" Pain hit Jesse's heart hard enough to make her gasp. She stopped. Those days, those dark days long ago were too painful to discuss. She shook her head. "I broke and she was there. She was more than I can say, and I hate knowing I have to live without her."

Silence swallowed the room. Just when it became unbearable, Paul broke the tension. "Did I ever tell you guys about me and Deidra dating the same guy?" And he went off on a story that had everyone laughing. As he talked, he walked around the room, engaging every person, gently touching Jesse's shoulder as he passed by the couch, buying her time.

Story after story was told, some making them laugh, some making them cry, every story drawing Deidra closer. One by one, friends drifted away to fall asleep on the most available bed or couch. One by one, the lights were turned off, until only a lamp here and there kept the rooms from being totally dark.

Deidra kept her place with Jesse and Connor, listening to their memories, growing stronger in their love for her. The bottle of brandy was finally empty. Jesse was asleep, her head on Connor's shoulder, his hand protectively covering hers. If sometime during the night Jesse's hand became someone else's, reaching out to actually touch Connor again, and if Jesse whispered, "I love you," in a low throaty voice that wasn't her own, who was to know?

CHAPTER 10

Connor woke up with a stiff neck and back. Jesse slept next to him, her forehead furrowed as if in thought. Connor realized with a start that he had thought Deidra was there. That he had thought she was holding his hand, she was saying his name. He shook off the dream with regret. Closing his eyes wasn't going to make it true.

All around the room, people slept in various poses, some fully clothed, some in boxers or bra and panties. Deidra hadn't chosen her friends for modesty or shyness. Connor had to acknowledge the appropriateness of this communal assortment. He tried to count the number of Jack Daniels bottles and lost track. They had done Deidra proud.

Slowly and gently, he placed a pillow under Jesse's head and got up. God, she looked tired. It was hard to imagine this girl as Deidra's best friend. They must have looked like Jeff and Mutt, Deidra eclipsing Jesse's tiny pale image with her vibrant presence. Maybe that was the point. Maybe Jesse liked disappearing in Deidra's shadow. Or maybe Deidra liked being magnified by Jesse's nondescript image. Maybe both. He would never know, of course.

Around the room, others started waking up, some groaning as they grabbed their heads, others fully cognizant when their eyes opened. One actress stumbled to the balcony in her underwear to light a cigarette. Sal sat up and immediately drained the last drop of whiskey from the bottle next to him. The awakening room ran like a silent film and Connor memorized it, filing it away in his creative brain for future use.

Bethany, Deidra's understudy, wearing only a black pushup bra and panties, stepped over bodies and encircled Connor's waist, resting her head against his shoulder. "So today we go on without her," Bethany said softly. Connor felt her hand run lightly up his back and stepped away. He felt his face flush. "I'll be there for you," Bethany continued, seeming not to notice

Connor's withdrawal. "Anytime, anywhere, Connor. I know this must be so hard for you." Bethany stepped close again and kissed him lightly on the mouth before walking away. "See you in New York."

Connor took a deep breath and composed himself. She didn't mean anything, he thought. I'm reading too much into it. "Thank you," he managed to say to Bethany's retreating back. She turned to throw a little smile over her shoulder. As she passed, Jesse, still sleeping by the couch, straightened out her leg and Bethany tripped over it, barely catching herself against a table and hitting hard enough to hurt. She grabbed her shin and rubbed, glaring angrily at Jesse, but Jesse slept on. Bethany's sensual sashay was reduced to a limping hop as she went in search of her clothes. Connor grinned. If Jesse hadn't been so sound asleep, Connor would have sworn the trip was intentional.

"Still looking out for Deidra?" Connor asked the sleeping Jesse. He quietly slipped into another room to join a small group. If Bethany had been suggesting anything, he wasn't going to make himself available for another one-on-one.

Suzanne and Jake looked up expectantly as Connor walked toward them. "Where's our girl?" Jake asked. "I thought she'd wake up by now. You guys had more staying power than the rest of us last night but still—Jesse's usually a light sleeper."

"Jesse doesn't usually drink whiskey," Suzanne laughed. "I'll get her."

"And brandy," Connor added. Jake and Suzanne raised their eyebrows but didn't say anything.

Connor was ready to leave by the time Suzanne returned, supporting an awake but still-groggy Jesse by the waist. "We need to get some coffee into this girl," Suzanne reported. "It took five minutes just to get her to open her eyes."

Jesse rubbed at her temples and sighed. "I have to stop drinking," she moaned. "I don't know how Deidra did it, but obviously I can't. I'm too tired to function, and God, my head."

"Wash up and then downstairs for breakfast," Suzanne insisted. "I understand they serve stale donuts and bagels along with watered-down coffee—if that doesn't wake you up, nothing will. You'll run screaming for the closest diner."

Jesse blanched at the mention of food. "I don't think I can eat anything," she groaned.

Suzanne frowned. "When was the last time you did eat, Jesse? You certainly didn't eat that swill they

86

served at the church, and I don't remember you having anything last night ...." Realization dawned on Suzanne's face. "Jesse, have you eaten since Deidra died? You haven't, have you? Come on." She grabbed Jesse's arm and pulled her, none too gently towards the bathroom. "Meet you guys downstairs in ten minutes," she ordered. "If they don't serve real food we're going somewhere that does."

"I have to go," Connor protested but Suzanne interrupted him.

"Not until we all have some breakfast," she said firmly. Connor nodded obediently. Suzanne was in charge, and having someone in charge right now was perfectly fine with him.

It was a subdued group that met in the dining room. To everyone's pleasant surprise, the buffet breakfast included fresh fruit, yogurt, scrambled eggs and a variety of other breakfast foods, all premade, all from frozen boxes, but edible. Suzanne piled a plate and set the food in front of Jesse, who only stared at it and shook her head.

"You have to eat, and we'll all sit here until you do. Come on, everyone, eat!' Suzanne lowered her voice to whisper into Jesse's ear, "If you don't eat, I'll feed you, Jesse. Now, mangia!" She picked up a fork of scrambled eggs and forced it between Jesse's closed lips.

Obediently, Jesse chewed and swallowed and was surprised to find out she was really, really hungry. She took the fork from Suzanne and smiled. "Oh, food—you mean 'eat *food*'! For a moment I thought you were making another pass."

Suzanne's eyebrows shot up, but she laughed. "A little risqué, for you, don't you think, Jesse? For a moment you sounded like ..."

Her comment was lost in the laughter around the room. Everyone seemed relieved to break away from the burden of grief and if a suggestive, out-of-character comment from Jesse was what it took they were ready to accept that. Suzanne didn't join in, but sat studying Jesse's face, which was registering something like surprise at her own joke.

"Hey, Suzanne! If she's not interested, I am," Tonya, a cast member, quipped bawdily. She batted her eyelashes extravagantly, winning another round of laughter.

Suzanne stole one more concerned glance at Jess and then rose to the occasion. She stood up, pulled Tonya to her feet and looked her up and down, slowly and rakishly, until even the dining room attendant stopped serving and stared. "I always did want to visit New York," Suzanne suggested, her voice dropping a register. "As you can see, Montrose just doesn't appreciate me." She slipped an arm around Tonya's waist and dipped her back over her arm, planting a kiss on the actress's lips. Tonya made an act of swooning, allowing her back to arch improbably as one leg rose and encircled Suzanne's thigh. Attendants gaped as Deidra's friends burst into applause and gave Suzanne and Tonya a standing ovation. It was only when the two broke apart to take deep bows that the staff members remembered to continue with their work, nervous smiles accentuating stiff, unnatural movement around the tables.

"It's alright, honey; we're artists," Sal reassured the girl clearing away his dish. "You know what we're like—anything goes." He blew her a kiss and she blushed furiously, obviously uncomfortable with his antics. He shrugged extravagantly and addressed the room, "I don't think she likes me." Laughter exploded again.

Conversation started around the room, flowing more naturally than it had any other time since Deidra's funeral. Connor noticed that when Jesse was laughing with her friends she was much prettier than he had originally thought, and as she bandied off- color comments and joined Jake in an impromptu tango to demonstrate lessons they had taken in college, he could see why Deidra had chosen this wisp of a girl to be her best friend. They were more alike than he could have imagined.

When the staff started breaking down the breakfast buffet, members of the group wandered away individually and in couples. Those who were headed for the bus in Scranton piled into rental cars. Unlike the previous day, the sun was shining, and warmth could be felt in the spring air.

Connor walked Jesse to her car, blocking her way as he held the door open for her. "I'm sorry that I accused you of writing on Deidra's wall," he said. "I was shocked and angry, and I couldn't think of anyone else who could have such a thing. Maybe it was Mary. I don't know, but I'm glad the second posting happened while you were right in front of me." He shook his head. "I'm going to stop them if I find out who it is."

"Why?" Jesse's shrugged. "If that's someone else's way to manage grief, what difference could it possibly make? God knows I'm not handling things well." She pulled Deidra's ring out of her pocket and held it out to him. "I wasn't even going to tell you I had this; then, when you turned it down I was totally relieved. Pretty selfish, don't you think? I'm offering again. Please, take it."

She thrust the ring toward him and he reverently accepted it, kissed it and slid it onto his little finger where it stopped above the knuckle. "Doesn't exactly fit," he smiled.

A sudden look of shock ran across Connor's face. He grabbed at the ring as if he couldn't get it off fast enough. "Goddamn!"

"What?" Jesse's voice registered her alarm. "What? Did I do something to it? Is something wrong?"

"I don't think I'm ready for this," Connor gasped. "I swear it felt like ice on my finger. A jolt ran up my arm so hard I thought I was having a heart attack." He grasped Jesse's hand, placed the ring firmly in her palm and closed her fingers over it. He stood holding onto her hand, patting it ever so gently. "Will you keep this for me for a while? I'm not saying I never want it, but I can't accept it right now and you're the only other person I think Deidra would want to have it. Please?"

Jesse was conflicted. For the past few days, she hadn't eaten, had been drunk or hung-over at all times, couldn't get through a night without seeing Deidra's ghost, had brushed off Brian and hadn't even considered going to work. Her head ached constantly and, unless Deidra's ghost was very, very real, she had done things without even knowing she was doing them, like throwing her clothes all over the room. At least she now knew for sure she wasn't the one posting on Facebook. Still, when she had handed Connor the ring, she had experienced a flash of lucidity that she hadn't had in days. She was even more convinced that the ring was connected with whatever was happening to her.

"Connor, do you believe in ghosts?" she asked suddenly. "I mean, have you ever seen a ghost? Seen Deidra's ghost?" She didn't know why she had asked him but somehow it made sense to her that if she could see Deidra, the one other person who could would be Connor.

He shook his head slowly. "I wish," he said.

Jesse slipped behind the wheel of her car. "Are you sure you want me to have this?" she asked again, opening her hand one more time to offer up Deidra's ring.

"For now," Connor said. He leaned down to kiss her lightly on the cheek and then put his arms around her, and hugged her tightly. "Stay in touch, okay?"

"Yes—you, too." Jesse dropped the ring back into her pocket and could have sworn, just for a moment, that it resisted falling there.

As Jesse pulled away in the car, Deidra reached for Connor. For one moment she had thought he knew she was there. He was supposed to take the ring, god damn it! What was this thing that happened when she touched anyone? God damn, Jesse! Why could she hug him when Deidra couldn't? It wasn't fair! Deidra aimed a blow at Jesse in pure jealous rage.

The sudden onslaught of pain in Jesse's chest was enough to nearly make her lose control of the car. Her head felt like it was splitting in two. She pulled off on the shoulder and waited for the jolt to subside. Her stomach rolled, threatening to reject the only food she'd had in days. For a change, she managed to get through the moment without vomiting. Whatever was going on with her, she had to get a grip. She just had to. Tears slid down her cheeks as sorrow flooded over and through her. No more smoking, no more drinking, no more ghosts. She vowed to go home, take a bath, get back to work—anything that would distract her from all of this craziness.

She rocked back and forth as she cried and Deidra cried with her. "I'm sorry, Jesse; so, so sorry," Deidra said. "I didn't mean it. Honest, I didn't. I'm just so lost."

CHAPTER 11

Suzanne was worried. As long as she had known Deidra and Jesse, Deidra had been the flamboyant one and Jesse had been almost painfully reserved. Even in their wildest moments, Jesse had held back.

Suzanne could remember one Halloween when the whole crew had tucked little dots of acid in their mouths to get the full affect of their grotesque costumes. While everyone else howled in delight at the hallucinations, Jesse had howled in fear. Jake and Suzanne had held her between them, talking to her until things calmed down. Deidra had said it was because Jesse couldn't let go of control without being terrified and they had all agreed to never put her in that spot again.

Hearing Jesse make sexual jokes—lesbian jokes at that—and watching Jesse dance the tango with Jake with an overt sexuality instead of the carefully memorized steps she had learned in college was so out of character that Suzanne couldn't quite accept it as being okay. And it certainly wasn't okay that Jesse had ended her tango with a saucy kick and flip of her skirt so much like—no—just like Deidra. It wasn't as good and it wasn't as polished, but it was there just the same, jerky and off balance, like Jesse was a puppet and someone was pulling her strings.

Whatever was going on, no one else seemed to notice it, but Suzanne did. And it wasn't funny. Suzanne turned around in Lenox and headed back to Montrose. Jesse had a spare room and Suzanne had decided she would stay for a couple of nights. If things were okay, no harm done. If not—she wasn't sure what she would do, but she was going to be there.

Brian's BMW smelled like coffee and Egg McMuffin. He checked his watch for the hundredth time only to see ten minutes had passed since the last time he'd checked. Where was she? He'd been sitting here how long? Two hours that felt more like twelve. He gathered the scattered pages of the Wall Street Journal and threw them into the back seat. It was time to give it up. *If she's not here in fifteen minutes I'm gone*, he told himself. But what if something had happened to her?

His fingers were turning the key when Jesse's yellow Volkswagen Beetle pulled up in front of the house. Finally! He wasn't sure what he wanted to say and wasn't even sure if she would talk to him, but the argument the night before was bothering him. He wasn't sure what worried him the most: Jesse sending him away or the reason she sent him away. Maybe he was just appalled that for a moment things had gotten physical, and not in a good way. Brian prided himself on never, ever being violent, and he was pretty sure that grabbing Jesse and her pushing him into the wall constituted violence.

Jesse got out of her car slowly and leaned against it, rubbing her temples. She looked awful. She still wore the dress from the night before but now the perfectly pressed linen was wrinkled as if she had slept in it. Her hair hadn't been brushed, and she dragged herself up the front steps holding on to the railing with one hand while dangling her purse from the other.

Jesse put her key in the lock and then leaned there against the door, collecting herself before turning the door knob. Brian's heart lurched as he saw what a gargantuan effort it was for Jesse to move.

Suddenly he wanted to carry her to bed and tuck her in. He wanted to make her hot tea and tell her he would take care of her until this—whatever it was— was over. His knotted stomach felt heavy. Why had he been such as ass? He slipped his keys into his pocket, reached for the door handle and then stopped.

A red Miata pulled up behind Jesse's car. Before it had even fully stopped, the door flew open as a young man rushed out. He was slight of build, much smaller than Brian himself. His hair was dark and short, neatly combed back. The white shirt and black suit were obviously tailored to fit the slim shoulders and hips perfectly. Even from a distance, in that split second Brian could see that he was handsome, almost effeminate, with his chiseled cheek and jaw bones.

The young man ran up the steps, slipped a protective arm around Jesse, pushed the door open, guided Jesse inside and closed the door behind them. Brian got just a glimpse of Jesse's arms going up and around the guy before the door shut.

Brian's face grew hot. His heart pounded against his chest wall. His fists clenched, unclenched and clenched again. So this was the reason Jesse had sent him away. She didn't need him—she needed that guy, whoever he was—maybe a past partner from college—a previous bed partner who had seen her with no underwear and shared a joint or pill or whatever they did at that school. Brian left tire marks on the macadam as he hit the gas, just barely missing the bumper of the car in front of him. His tires squealed resistance as he pushed the pedal to the floor, veering around the quick turn onto Church Street and up Public Ave.

He can have her, whoever he is. Brian had had enough.

Suzanne was totally unaware of Brian's scrutiny. She would have found his assessment of her humorous and very flattering. It took a lot of effort to be the best looking guy in the room, and she spent a great deal of money doing it.

But all Suzanne saw when she arrived at Jesse's was the way Jesse looked so beaten. Dark circles of exhaustion stood out under her eyes. Suzanne wrapped an arm around Jesse's waist just as

Jesse lost whatever strength she had left and started slipping down the door. "Brian?"

"Not even close," Suzanne answered.

A wave of gratitude swept over Jesse as Suzanne murmured, "Hang in there, Jesse. I've got you." She crumpled, putting her arms around Suzanne to keep from falling.

A kitchen chair was the closest seat. Suzanne guided Jesse gently to it and eased her down. "You have some good tea in this house or just those stupid tea bags?" Suzanne asked briskly.

"Cha-Cha Chai in the silver canister," Jesse pointed in the vague direction of the counter top and laughed, "You're pretty picky you know. What are you doing here? Not that I don't want to see you—God knows I do—but what are you doing here anyway?"

"I'm your knight in shining armor," Suzanne laughed, "and you need one, Sweetie. Let's see—oh yeah—the tea pot." Suzanne went through the drawers until she found a tea screen, pulled a white English bone china pot, decorated with roses, from its display shelf on the wall and took translucent cups from the cupboard. *This chick knows her tea.* She filled the kettle with water and set it to boil. She measured out enough dry leaves not for one pot, but for two pots of tea. She did all this without asking permission or assistance and, when everything was ready, she hung her sports coat carefully over the back of a chair, rolled up her sleeves and muddled cream, sugar and a shot of whiskey in each cup. Suzanne's fingers drummed impatiently on the counter top until the whistle screamed that the water was boiling. She filled the tea pot, placed it in the middle of the table on a lace heat pad and sat down with a complacent sigh.

Jesse watched the whole procedure, gradually going from exhausted to amused, finally laughing outright when Suzanne took the seat across from her. "Now that's what I like about women," Jesse chuckled. "Men offer to help but women just do it. Perfect."

"Okay, then," Suzanne put on her most serious interview face and looked Jesse in the face, holding Jesse's gaze firmly with her own. "You are going to tell me what the hell is going on; why instead of showing up at Deidra's funeral to cry a few tears, tell a few stories and go home, you showed up shaking like a leaf, unfed and withdrawn. Then you proceeded to drink like a fish and get smutty on me. It's not like you, Jesse." Suzanne leaned back in her chair and waited.

Minutes dragged by without any conversation. The hot tea and whiskey burned Jesse's throat at first, then settled as a warm glow in her stomach. She could feel her neck muscles relax and her lungs expand as if she'd been holding her breath for a long, long time. Suzanne watched with relief as Jesse's face went from white to rosy. Jesse's mind traced back to the moment she first saw Deidra on the bus, and a low groan started somewhere in her toes and spread upward, finally slipping from her lips. Suzanne didn't try to stop her and didn't try to comfort her. She just waited.

Finally, Jesse fell quiet. She pushed her cup toward Suzanne for a refill and sipped the strong tea slowly. "I found her, you know," she said softly.

It was Jesse's voice, quiet and subdued, but very much the Jesse Suzanne knew.

"Mary told us," Suzanne said. "Must have been rough."

"I went nuts. The cops and bus driver had to pull me away and force me to leave and all the time I was screaming 'No, no, no,' and holding on to Deidra's ring."

"You had Deidra's ring? What ring?"

"The engagement ring that Connor gave her. I didn't know I had it. I was so crazy they didn't know what to do with me. Thank god, Brian was in the car and heard the ruckus. They let him bring me home. He stayed a while."

"A while?" Suzanne felt the first stirring of anger start somewhere inside and took a deep breath. This was no time to talk. It was time to listen. "He didn't stay the night? "

Tears welled in Jesse's eyes for a moment but she brushed them away and set her mouth in a grimace. "Men, you know. They don't take well to big emotional scenes. I mean, they want to comfort and all that, but having failed once that's the end of it. Anyway, we talked, I cried, I got hysterical, I started drinking Deidra's whiskey …"

"Deidra's whiskey?" Suzanne raised her eyebrows. "How'd that go?"

"You know how it went. I hadn't been making much sense in the first place and before long I was making no sense at all. At some point Brian put me in bed and left. He said I 'needed some space.' Asshole."

"Cheers to that," Suzanne laughed and raised her tea cup in a salute.

They sipped in agreement and Jesse continued. "And then I woke up." She grew silent, twirling the cup around and around. "Suzanne?"

"Hum?"

"Have you ever seen a ghost?"

Now we're getting somewhere, Suzanne thought. "I haven't," she said, "but that doesn't mean I don't believe anyone else has."

"Deidra was here. That night. She didn't know she was dead. She kept saying she was cold and putting on her sweater." Jesse's voice was flat— emotionless. "She threw my clothes all over my room."

"She what?" Suzanne stared at Jesse in disbelief and Jesse pushed her chair back angrily.

"You don't believe me either." Her tone was louder, edged with what Suzanne was starting to recognize as hysteria and something else …fear?

"I didn't say that, Jesse. Just give me a moment. Now, you saw her throw your clothes?"

"Yes. She was looking for the sweater and she threw everything all over my room. That's what woke me up!"

"You told Brian?"

"And he said I did it, of course. Crazy little drunk Jesse ransacked her room and blamed it on a ghost. But I didn't do it, did I? And then I was cleaning up the mess the next day and that's when I found the ring, and I tried to give it Connor but he wouldn't take it and I didn't want him to and Brian and I had a big fight and Deidra wrote on the computer and … I'm getting this mixed up. Deidra wrote on the computer and Connor called me in the middle of the night and called me a bitch … a fucking bitch … and then…Oh, God, Suzanne, I'm going crazy, aren't I? I can't sleep but I can't wake up and my head hurts all the time and no one believes me. And now you don't believe me either…" Jesse's words got lost in renewed sobbing. Suzanne ran around the table and grabbed Jesse's hands just as she drew back her arm to throw the tea cup across the room.

"Hush. Hush. I didn't say I didn't believe you. It's alright. It's going to be alright now."

"Suzanne," Jesse hiccupped, "I didn't really want Connor to take the ring and I didn't want Brian to come back because if I did … if they did … she wouldn't come back, would she? And I don't want her to be gone." Suzanne kept her arms around Jesse until she could feel Jesse's body collapse against her.

"If I let go are you going to smash that fabulous tea pot?"

"No. I think I'm done smashing things."

"Okay then."

Suzanne sat back down and Jesse pulled her chair back to the table and they sat quietly in their own thoughts while minutes ticked by.

"Where is it?" Suzanne finally asked.

"It?"

"The ring."

"Oh." Jesse searched through her pockets and pulled it out. Suzanne held it to the light, turning it around.

"Nice rock," Suzanne said appreciatively. She slipped it on and admired her hand. "The guy has some serious bucks, even if he does look like a pauper. This is one fine ring."

Deidra watched Suzanne put on the ring with puzzlement. When Jesse and Connor had touched the ring, Deidra had been able to access them as easily as water flowing into an empty glass. When Suzanne put on the ring Deidra couldn't touch her. Something in Jesse and Connor called to her, willed her to come to them and she was happy to go, but Suzanne—with a jolt Deidra realized that Suzanne didn't call her at all. Even when Suzanne studied the ring and held it to the light, nothing pulled Deidra to her. Deidra experimented, tentatively at first and then boldly, touching Suzanne, putting her arms around her and finally even trying to thrust her hand into Suzanne's. Nothing; not even that shiver that Deidra had come to expect as a reaction. It was something to think about. Finally Deidra gave up, nestling back down into the ring to watch.

"It doesn't bother you?" Suzanne noticed the look of surprise on Jesse's face and laughed.

"Why should it bother me?"

"Well, Connor acted like he'd been burned when he put it on, and when I touch it …When I touch it, it kind of…burns, but cold burn, if you know what I mean…and it's heavy or something. I can't explain."

Suzanne slipped it off and put it next to the tea pot. "It doesn't bother me except for the fact that I don't think anyone is ever going to give me one."

Laughter escaped from Jesse and lay between them like a warm blanket. Suzanne was pleased. This might be a hard conversation, but it was a good one. She thought it was helping.

"You know, I think you should take a bath and get out of that dress and into some nice sweats. Then we'll talk about something else."

"Like what."

"Like the girl from the tennis team who made me who I am today," Suzanne offered in a low, suggestive voice. "I know you're curious. Everyone is. But I'm going to explain it in graphic detail right after you smell better. Deal?"

"Deal, but don't think you're going to corrupt me. Brian thinks I'm corrupt enough."

"He would."

Jesse pushed herself away from the table. For the first time in days, she didn't take the ring with her. "Thanks," she smiled at Suzanne and went upstairs to run a bath.

CHAPTER 12

Jesse slipped further down in the claw-foot tub. Hot bath water massaged her tired muscles. She slapped absent-mindedly at the bubbles, which tickled across her nose and chin. She let her mind float away from her with no focus whatsoever.

Suzanne was somewhere in the house doing something or nothing—whatever. The knowledge made her feel safe. She listened, but she could only hear silence. Nice. She pictured Suzanne in her beautifully tailored suit. *How on earth did she keep that suit immaculate and what the hell did she do with her boobs? I know she had some.* Jesse realized she didn't know what time it was, and that she didn't care. Fatigue crept through her and she concentrated on the way the warm water was washing pain away. At some point, her head stopped trying to rip itself open. Finally, she slept.

Deidra's release from Jesse's sub-consciousness had a shocking effect on Deidra. She felt like she was a helium balloon and someone had cut the string. She floated away into silence. In a panic she clung to the ring, wondering what would happen to her without Jesse grounding her.

There had been stories about people going to the light— passing-over—yeah, that's what they called it. She looked frantically around to see if some vortex was opening up to suck her into—what?—heaven or some such place. They'd make her sing an unending "Hallelujah Chorus" and wear some non-descript white gown while bowing eternally to one God or another. And what if she hadn't decided on one God but sort of had faith in all of them? Was she going to burn in hell for not putting a name on her faith? Were Jehovah and Buddha and Allah going to gang up together and send her into some type of hell or other because she hadn't ever found one of them to be any better than the other? Because she had held forth, loudly and clearly, on the virtue of each and the impossibility of believing in just one of them?

Deidra remembered the crow at her funeral saying, "You know, death has very little to do with living—unless you want it to."

"I don't want it to! I don't want it to!" Deidra insisted.

But there wasn't any light, no bright tunnel, no swirling vortex, and little by little Deidra relaxed. Okay, then. The crow had been right; or kind of right, because death sure was making a lot of changes in her concept of living.

Off in the quiet of wherever and whatever this was, Deidra relaxed her hold on the ring. It would hold on to her, she realized. She didn't need to hold on to it. She relaxed in the void around her and had another revelation. She was tired. She was exhausted from everything she had done and been through and wanted nothing more than to sink into this oblivion and sleep. And that's exactly what she did.

"Wake up, Princess. You're turning into a prune."

"Leave me alone. I'm tired." Jesse tried to shut out Suzanne's no-nonsense voice and go back to sleep.

"Your lips are turning blue and there's a horny lesbie staring at your woo-woo. Get up."

Jesse struggled to consciousness and sat up. The tub water was tepid. Goose bumps covered her arms and chest, turning them into coarse sandpaper. Tremors ran through her body and chattered her teeth.

"How long have I been asleep?" Something was kinked in her neck. She turned her head side to side, waiting for the click that would tell her everything was back in place. In front of her, a six-foot tall towel stood waiting. All that could be seen of Suzanne was her feet and her hands.

"You can't see anything through that, horny or not," Jesse observed but she pushed herself to a standing position and let Suzanne help her out of the tub and wrap her in terry cloth from head to toe, expertly hitching it up and winding it into a sarong around Jesse's tiny frame.

"You really are too short to be a grown up," Suzanne teased, "Time to put some clothes on."

She pushed Jesse through the bathroom door toward the bedroom.

"How did you get so good at this?"

"Practice makes perfect, although most of the women I take such tender care of are a little more appreciative than you seem to be."

"Woo-woo?" Jesse asked and then blushed. "Never mind."

"Right," Suzanne said with a laugh. "Glad to see you're awake. And by the way—some guy has called about a hundred times asking if you filed the extension for Big Dog Construction. That's some redneck's phallic image I suppose?"

It was too much. Jesse burst into laughter not only because Suzanne was outrageous, but because Gary Billings probably did see himself as the "Big Dog" in more ways than one. He'd certainly made it clear that he could be her big dog if she wanted him to be. Finessing rednecks was a required skill in Susquehanna County.

Jesse pulled on comfortably worn-out sweats and moved out to the front porch, curling into the oversize white wicker rocker while Suzanne, dressed in perfectly ironed khakis and a polo shirt, which was about as dressed down as she ever got, sat on the matching love seat, .

Suzanne shivered and pulled a plaid wool throw around her shoulders. "Does it ever get warm here?"

"For about two weeks in July," Jesse replied. "You'll notice I don't have a swimming pool."

Suzanne surveyed the large sloping yard dotted with flowering fruit trees and blooming perennials. "You have no idea what this would cost in Philadelphia. I'm lucky to have a balcony. When was this built?"

"1835." Jesse felt a sense of satisfaction as she took in the manicured lawn and the view of the small town."

"Pre-Civil War? This isn't part of the underground railroad, is it?"

"Some say yes, some say no. But I found what look like old tunnels under the house, and that," Jesse pointed down the hill to her left, "is where the freemen built their church and school. I wouldn't be surprised if they hid in the tunnels when the Fugitive Slave Act was enacted. Slave catchers could legally come looking for runaways and pretty much claimed anyone and everyone with dark skin was an escaped slave."

"I'm surprised you haven't seen more ghosts before now."

Suzanne bit her lip, sorry she'd mentioned ghosts, but Jesse just laughed. "I try not to see them."

Jesse's statement took Suzanne completely by surprise. "Try not to see them?"

"My mother always said, 'Places aren't haunted; people are.' She was one of those people who could connect, you know? I found out at a very young age that I could do it, too. We were alike that way. And it doesn't stop with ghosts. Sometimes something is going to happen and I know about it beforehand. The phone rings and I know who's on the other end and what they're going to say. I knew when my sister lost her baby three hundred miles away. There have been lots of things. It's hard to explain."

"That kind of knowledge could drive you crazy."

"It did. I've learned to shut it out, or at least I try to, but now ..." Jesse let out a long sigh. "Do you remember when I fell apart at school and Deidra stood by me? No one understood what was going on, but Deidra did. She saved me."

"Well, she's driving you crazy now."

"No. What's driving me crazy is the fact that I don't want to let her go. She needs me and ... without her I'll be lost."

"People die, Jesse." Suzanne hadn't meant to sound so harsh. "I'm sorry," she added quickly.

Suzanne didn't want to dwell on Deidra, but Jesse wouldn't let it go. "I was a photography major. I got it in my head that I should do an exhibit of old graveyards—you know—like the Brookdale Cemetery. I couldn't get a clean shot. Every one of them had these round spots. It drove me crazy."

"Dirty lens," Suzanne said, "happens all the time."

"That's what I thought, so I switched cameras. And it still happened. Do you know what orbs are?"

"Circles, lights, balls, right?"

"Pictures of dead spirits. There are people who dedicate their lives to capturing an orb. I can't get away from them. They look like lint on the lens or maybe a drop of water, dust in the air, something. "

Suzanne was losing patience with Jesse's ghost fascination. Maybe the girl was really crazy, at least in this area. But still, if something was wrong, wasn't she here to listen? "Okay, so what made you decide they were orbs instead of dirt? Give me some proof."

"I was using a digital SLR. I never had that problem with my manual but the digital—well, it was different. If I'd been using good-old black-and-white film I'm not sure if the same thing would have happened. Anyway, Deidra and I went to Gettysburg because there are graveyards all over the place, and everyone says they're haunted. Pretty cool, right? Except my pictures kept having those spots, and Deidra's didn't. She wasn't even good with a camera but she was getting all these cool shots, and I was frantic because I couldn't afford to replace the lenses in my camera and it was practically brand new, for Pete's sake!

"Anyway, we decided to switch cameras. We agreed not to mess with any of the settings—just snap with what the other one had been using. Mine came out with orbs and Deidra's came out crystal clear."

"So something in your clothes," Suzanne insisted.

"Except Deidra thought my anger and frustration was funny, so she turned and snapped a picture of me being pissed off. I was surrounded by orbs. They were over, beside, in front of … everywhere. I was a regular ghost magnet."

"Jesse, I'm not buying it. You were standing in a dust cloud. Deidra didn't do you any favors going along with that."

"Don't bad mouth Deidra or we can't talk, okay?"

Suzanne nodded.

"Okay then. The biggest problem was that I could hear them. The longer I stood there, the louder they got. I could hear whispers, cries. It shook me to the bone. Something touched my hand, and the ice that went up my arm scared me so much I grabbed Deidra and she dropped my camera. It shattered. I didn't buy another one. I just stopped taking pictures, then and ever after."

Suzanne thought for a minute, trying to make herself believe. She couldn't. "Okay, so did you know that Deidra was going to die? If you know things why was that such a surprise?"

"I don't know." Jesse's voice had dropped to a whisper. "I didn't know when my mother was going to die either. Deidra was coming to see me. If I had known …" Her voice trailed off. When she spoke again it was in a whisper. "She called me from Port Authority. I could have told her not to come. I feel guilty for not knowing. I should have felt something!"

Suzanne had had enough. "I think that if you would accept that Deidra is dead you might be able to get on with your life. I also know that this conversation isn't going to keep the ghosts at bay and I, for one, am not ready, willing or able to visit with anyone who isn't currently alive and kicking. So, let's talk about how you're going to save me a bundle in taxes this year. And," Suzanne put on a heavy scowl and shook her finger at Jesse, "please don't tell me if I'm going to die in a car wreck on the way home."

"Good Lord," Jesse groaned. "I don't want to know any such thing. Your wish is my command. We'll change the subject." Suzanne let out an exaggerated sigh of relief and was rewarded with a laugh from Jesse.

They talked about work and decorating and finances and tax shelters. Whenever the conversation started gravitating toward Deidra, Suzanne moved it in another direction. The more they talked about things unrelated to Deidra and their college days the healthier Jesse looked, and that was exactly what Suzanne wanted.

Time after time, Suzanne made Jesse laugh without realizing she was being funny. She suggested they have dinner delivered and Jesse gave her a startled look, as if it was a foreign idea, before reaching out to pat Suzanne's hand and remind her that "we're not in Kansas anymore, Dorothy."

Neither felt like getting dressed to go out, so they made do with some canned asparagus and cold shrimp. "I have ice cream and popcorn," Jesse reassured Suzanne, "both of which go well with chardonnay or blackberry brandy and tea."

If Suzanne couldn't understand why Jesse stayed in the little nowhere town that didn't have something as basic as pizza delivery, she understood when night fell. The moon was only a sliver and, without street lights to obscure them, stars filled the sky. Jesse pointed out various constellations and the planet Venus. Suzanne hadn't seen stars since moving to Philadelphia, and had never seen stars like these.

She was even more captivated when Jesse helped her carry her suitcase and hanging clothes to the third floor of the house. Jesse had done a fantastic job renovating. The original wood moldings, doors and stairs gleamed, and the guest suite was magical with an antique brass bed, occasional tables, and an old-fashioned claw tub in a private bath. Suzanne sat herself in the upholstered window seat, gazed out at the stars overhead and the town lights below and swore she wasn't leaving. "I'll just plug in my computer at that lovely little desk and you can send me meals in the dumbwaiter. You do have a dumbwaiter, I assume?"

"I do," Jesse agreed, "and you are welcome to stay as long as you like. Except I'm not cooking for you after a week or so, so the best you're going to get is a pot of tea or coffee."

"Deal. Maybe I'll change careers and start a business delivering for the local restaurants. You do have local restaurants, don't you?"

For an answer Jesse threw a fresh towel at her. "We're not totally uncivilized, you know. We are the County Seat and not only have restaurants but a library, book store, grocery store, post office and one bar for every church, of which there are many."

"My kind of town," Suzanne sighed. "What about night clubs?"

"If you like karaoke," Jesse laughed, "karaoke and beer."

"Oh, God, I'd die here."

"You would," Jesse agreed, "and with your wonderful advertising background you'd probably even be able to make what—$10.50 an hour?"

"Get out," Suzanne ordered. "You've burst my country fantasy. I'm going back to Philly and if you're smart you'll go with me."

"Don't think I haven't considered it. Sleep tight. Let me know if you need anything."

But Suzanne didn't go to bed. She listened while Jesse went down to the second floor; heard her wash up and go into her room. When the house was absolutely still, Suzanne tiptoed down the stairs and into Jesse's room. She settled herself into the reading chair and fell into a fitful doze. If Deidra was going to make an appearance, Suzanne wanted to make sure Jesse didn't slip back into the frightened mouse she had been this morning.

CHAPTER 13

Deidra had been focused on Jesse and never considered the possibility that she had options. She had clung to the ring and Jesse, and failed to recognize that, in clinging to them, she was limiting herself to their vicinity. While Suzanne worked on disconnecting Jesse from Deidra, Deidra was finding a new freedom when disconnected from Jesse.

At first, Deidra floated in limbo. She was now pretty sure that not all, but at least some of the time, lapses were naps. Like a newborn baby, she had been through the exhausting experience of birth and needed lots of rest. Now she napped longer and harder, but instead of frightening her it refreshed her.

At some point, she was again aware of voices around her, indistinct and inconsistent, but voices nonetheless. She no longer heard only cries of panic and fear but what might be conversations and laughter. She searched through dense fog to see where the voices were coming from, but it was hard to focus. It was kind of like flip, flip, flipping through TV or radio stations but never getting a clear signal. If dying was the equivalent of being born, was this process, learning to hear and understand, the same as a baby learning to speak or walk? *Potty training again*, she thought, *I was late at potty training.* The idea helped her relax and she worked to just observe and stop struggling with what was around her.

Now that she wasn't clinging and being clung to, she had a sensation she could only identify as a pull, or maybe a fall, in other directions. When she concentrated on her mother's voice, she found herself in her own childhood bedroom. At first, she wondered if she had done some time traveling. This wasn't the room she had visited during college or later on when she had moved to New York. The ruffled pink bedspread from her earliest memories was on the bed with matching pillow shams. Every doll she had ever owned was sitting on the pillows. The book shelves that had housed Stephen King and John Irving novels were now filled with Dr. Seuss, Old Mother Goose and Judy Blume. Even the clothes in the closet had changed. There was her Christening dress, a polka dot skirt she had worn when? Her first birthday?

She found herself in the hallway surrounded by pictures—a gallery of her life. But wait—these weren't just baby pictures. Here was her high school graduation, college graduation, her first play. So she wasn't time traveling.

And then she was in her mother's room and there was Mary, sitting absolutely still in the same rocking chair she had sat in when singing Deidra to sleep. "Mom? Mom, I'm here." But Mary didn't react. She stared at the wall, her lips moving without sound. In her hands, she held a bottle of Ambien. Deidra could tell from the date on the label that it was a new prescription. The bottle was full. As Deidra watched, her mother put two in her mouth and poured three more into her palm.

"No!" Deidra knocked the bottle onto the floor. Mary's shocked face stared at it in dismay, but she didn't move. As carefully as she could, Deidra knelt at her mother's feet and put her arms around Mary's waist. "I'm here, Mom. I'm here. I love you."

Some part of Mary understood. Her eyes became alert. Her breathing sped up as she stared at the pills rolling across the floor. "Oh my god!" she whispered. "What am I doing? What would Deidra say?"

Deidra tightened her grasp on her mother and held on. She swore she could touch her mother, stroke her hair, touch her face. She wasn't sure until Mary's questioning, "Deidra?" told her that Mary did, indeed, know she was there … and then a pull so strong she couldn't resist took her away even as she reached out. "Mom! Mom!"

She was in a bar she had gone to with Connor, his pull on her an intoxicated yearning—black and fierce. Next to him, Bethany sat with her arms around his waist, her lips whispering against his ear. *You can understudy me all you want, Bitch. You never could and never will be able to replace me,* Deidra snarled. Connor was too drunk to hear her, but the way Bethany jerked her head around told Deidra that Bethany might have heard or at least felt something. Deidra satisfied herself with a nudge of the glass of red wine and smiled as it tipped from the bar onto Bethany's all-too-exposed chest and ran like blood down the white spandex dress. Bethany jumped from her bar stool and ran for the ladies room. Connor didn't even notice. Deidra kissed his cheek and moved on, heartbroken as he turned toward her, puzzled and unfocused. "Deidra?" He shook his head and turned back to his drink.

She was on Houston Street, in front of the theater. The marquee still showed her face, but now a wide ribbon ran across it: "Rest in Peace, Deidra." Underneath it, bouquets rotted on the street—piles of them. A new picture featured Bethany, her face smiling out at passersby. Deidra slashed at it and it ripped. A middle-aged couple who had been reading the show announcements gawked as pieces fluttered to the sidewalk. Deidra was pulled away again.

Her high school corridor, where an early painting she had done still hung on the wall, the college campus, the corner store near her mother's house—she was thrown from one to another without any control at all until she was sure she was lost. She had to get back to Jesse. She had to get a grip on this crazy roller coaster.

One moment she felt in control, able make a conscious choice; the next moment she was ripped away to another place, another person. Her travels gleamed like cobwebs around her. She wondered if the web was a road she could follow later.

The web grew larger and flimsier as Deidra was yanked from place to place. With shock, she felt herself dissipating, becoming less and less real as she spread herself thinner. *No! Not yet!* She screamed. Her spirit was exhausted, used up. She still hadn't learned to move at will, and in every new place she left a part of herself. Fear made her panic; fear of becoming too insubstantial to pull herself together again.

She struggled to gather the fragments. She cried out Jesse's name and the pieces, all of those pieces pulling at her, came together. Sudden elation swept through her. She could travel. Maybe not so far at one time, but she could travel. With relief, she heard Jesse cry out, "Deidra!" and welcomed the pull that took her back—back to the safety of Jesse and the comforting confinement of the ring.

Jesse was dreaming. Deidra was lost and Jesse was looking for her. If Jesse didn't find her they were going to bury her. Finally, Deidra was just ahead, dodging between the trees at the cemetery in a black slip and red lipstick. She was laughing, waiting just until Jesse had her, could almost grab her, and then

Deidra was gone. For some reason Deidra couldn't see the hole or the people dressed in black gathered around it. She didn't hear the minister finishing the Lord's Prayer. "For Thine is the kingdom and the power and the glory forever. Amen."

The minister stepped back as Deidra ran across the graveyard. She turned to laugh at Jesse and fell backward into the hole. In the dream Jesse could see Deidra fall and fall and fall and then Jesse was falling with her, holding out her hand, trying to reach Deidra and save her but the fall got faster and faster. The fall became a vortex sucking them in and then they were not only falling but spinning. Every time Jesse almost had her, almost caught the long white arm, Deidra fell further away, laughing on and on. And then she was gone and Jesse couldn't see her anymore and she couldn't stop spinning and falling herself. "Deidra!"

Jesse's cry woke Suzanne, who fell from the chair where she had taken watch. Confused, Suzanne struggled to remember where she was and what she was doing there. A gust of wind caught her by surprise, and then another. In the dark Suzanne searched for a light switch, a lamp, anything. Suddenly the room lit up as the computer screen strobed. The wind intensified. Drawers of Jesse's dresser slammed in and out, in and out. The wind was actually howling through the room now, even though the window was closed. Pictures on Jesse's bedroom wall moved, slowly at first, and then in a rattling swing, pulling against their hooks. One picture, a black-and-white of Deidra poised on the stage on Houston Street, broke from its hook and didn't fall but rather spun in the air—a whirling top. It spun around and around while Suzanne fought the urge to run screaming from the room.

Suzanne crab-walked backwards to the wall. The strobing screen, blowing wind and twirling picture made her dizzy, knocked her off balance. She closed her eyes, finally blocking out enough sensation to find the light switch on the wall and flip it on.

Immediately she regretted being able to see. Jesse stood in the middle of the floor, her hypnotized eyes glued to the picture of Deidra. Slowly, ever so slowly she lifted her arms, pointed her toes and started to dance. She sashayed in front of the mirror, thrust her pelvis suggestively, threw back her head and laughed. For a grand finale she gave a saucy little kick, flipped up her night shirt to expose a very bare ass and blew Suzanne a kiss.

The computer stopped, the wind stopped, the picture fell to the floor with a shower of breaking glass and Jesse stood in the middle of the floor, confusion spreading across her features as she became aware. As realization hit, tears simply fell in sheets down her face. She stared at Suzanne helplessly. "It happened again, didn't it? I did something."

Suzanne opened her mouth and discovered she couldn't quite get words to come out. Finally she took a deep breath and managed to say, "No. No, Jesse, unless you think it's awful to dance. I do believe Deidra has paid us a visit."

Deidra was so relieved to be back in one piece, so excited to finally know what she could do, that she hadn't given any thought to the effect of her exuberance on Jesse. But it had been rather fun to see the cool unresponsive Suzanne crawl across the floor. Didn't believe in ghosts indeed. Ha! She had so much to learn. With a satisfied smile she wrapped herself up in the cocoon of the ring and rested.

CHAPTER 14

"Mr. Carpenter?"

Brian hit the button connecting him to his secretary with impatience. "I'm in a meeting, Kelly."

"I know, and I'm sorry, but she said it's urgent; she's very insistent."

The vice president of Capitol Gas and Oil, sitting across the polished desk from Brian, raised his eyebrows and offered a sympathetic smile. "I need to check in with the office anyway. Shall we say," he glanced at his watch, "fifteen minutes?"

Brain nodded as he reached for the phone and noticed with relief that Mr. Brant took neither the proposal nor his brief case with him when he left the room, quietly closing the door behind him. This particular endowment would mean saving the library, and Brian felt the weight of obligation almost suffocate him. He had to bring this money in.

Brian took a second to adjust his tone before connecting to the call. "Brian Carpenter. May I help you?"

"Brian?" He didn't recognize the female voice although she sounded like she knew him.

"Yes."

"My name is Suzanne Doyle. I'm a friend of Jesse's."

"Suzanne, I really can't really talk right now. Is Jesse alright?"

"Nice of you to ask," the voice was instantly hard, withdrawn. "No, she's not alright, but I've been here for a day and a half and you haven't shown up so I guess I should have known better than to call. Give me a ring back when you can talk."

Brian could hear the finality in Suzanne's voice and spoke quickly before she could disconnect. "Wait. Please wait. Why did you call?"

An exasperated sigh was followed by a long silence. Brian was pretty sure Suzanne had hung up and was relieved when she spoke again. "I need backup," she said. The strong, professional tone had softened. Was she crying? "It's hard to explain on the phone. I think you need to come over and see for yourself. "

"See what for myself? I'm truly stuck here for now—it's important."

This time the line really did go dead. Brian held the receiver to his ear and listened to the dial tone. Shit! What was he supposed to do now? Who was Suzanne anyway? He knew Jesse was having trouble dealing with Deidra's death but she had brushed him off over and over and there was that guy—whoever he was—he'd seen the day before.

Robert Brant of Capitol Gas and Oil returned in exactly fifteen minutes, smelling of cigarette smoke and breath mints and their meeting continued. If Brian seemed preoccupied Mr. Brant didn't mention it, but when Brian made the obligatory offer to continue their conversation over a late lunch it was declined. Brian had no idea how things stood when they shook hands and parted.

"If you need me, call my cell," Brian instructed Kelly and nearly ran to his car. It was less than a mile to Jesse's house. Brian said a short prayer that the one-and-only town cop was otherwise occupied as he sped past the courthouse and screeched through the only stop light in town. He hesitated for a second when he saw the red Miata still parked behind Jesse's car, but only for a second; the sense of urgency that had been building ever since Suzanne's call made him run up the steps to the front door. The shock at having the door opened by the handsome man he'd seen the day before pulled him up short. "Oh. Excuse me … I mean, I thought Jesse was expecting me."

"Brian?" Her familiar voice stopped him before he could turn and run back down the steps and away. "It sure took you long enough."

"Suzanne?"

A slow smile spread across the man's face. He opened the door wider and stepped aside, obviously intending for Brian to come in. Brian hesitated. The man chuckled and to Brian's amazement started unbuttoning his perfectly pressed white shirt.

Brian backed away but a slender brown hand reached out to stop him. The shirt opened, revealing a white guinea tee, which slid up to reveal a sports bra. Before Brian could even register what was coming next, the sports bra was lifted up, revealing two small but very female breasts. "Yes—I'm Suzanne."

Brian felt the heat of blood rushing to his cheeks and Suzanne laughed. "The first fun I've had in four days," she said, and quickly, efficiently pulled her

135

clothes back in place. "I do believe you thought Jesse was cheating," she laughed. "Trust me, she's not. She's a little bit crazy, but not that crazy."

"Okay. You got me," Brian acknowledged with a rueful grin and allowed himself to be pulled into the living room. "So why did you call?"

As an answer, Suzanne jerked her head toward the stairs. Brian followed obediently, dread building with every step. Whatever he had imagined didn't compare with what he saw.

Suzanne pushed the door of Jesse's room open and inclined her head toward the woman sitting in the reading chair. Jesse hadn't changed out of her nightgown. She sat curled up in the chair, cradling a bottle of whiskey. Now and then she took a deep swig.

"What happened?" There had to be an explanation, and he was pretty sure Suzanne could give a more coherent statement than Jesse right now.

"It seems that Deidra can break pictures, blow stuff around and even get our lady here to dance in true burlesque fashion."

"You don't believe that."

'I saw it," Suzanne stated flatly, "and no, until then, I didn't believe it."

Suzanne took the bottle away from Jesse and set it on the night table. Jesse frowned at her, struggling to focus her eyes, and tried to hang on to the bottle. "Come on, Ms. Drunkard. You've got company."

"Jesse?" Brian asked hesitantly and caught his breath at the look of happiness that flooded Jesse's face at the sound of his voice.

"Brian!" Without warning, Jesse jumped from the chair and stumbled to him. She threw her arms around him and sobbed into his neck while he struggled for balance. "Brian," Jesse said again, her voice muffled by his jacket. "I thought you'd never come."

He cradled her, petted her hair, whispered her name. "It's okay," he said, much as Suzanne had said the day before. He felt Jesse shudder and then relax, falling against him. "What should I do?" he asked Suzanne, who was still kneeling on the floor and watching them.

Whatever doubts Suzanne had had about Brian washed away with the fear, compassion and helplessness she saw on his face. "Get her out of here," she said. "We'll talk later but for now just get her away." So he did.

He sat Jesse gently back down in the chair and swiveled it to face the mirror.

"I don't feel so good," Jesse slurred. "I think I drank too much."

"It'll be alright." Gently, ever so gently, Brian brushed her hair. Then he got a warm cloth and washed her face. Suzanne smiled to see that Brian never even attempted to apply makeup, but rather kissed Jesse lightly on the cheek and smiled at her reflection. "There's my pretty lady." Suzanne left the room while Brian helped Jesse dress. They finally appeared in the living room, Brian still in his suit for work but Jesse in comfortable jeans and a sweatshirt.

"We'll walk to the Summerhouse Grill. If you don't mind, I'd like you to meet us there in a hour or so and tell me what happened here." Brian went into the kitchen and reappeared with a bottle of wine. "Bring your own booze," he explained to Suzanne's questioning look. "She doesn't need it, but I have a feeling I might."

Jesse wasn't saying much but looked more like herself than she had at any point since her nighttime dance as Deidra. Suzanne felt relief wash over her. Until now, she had been afraid that Jesse really was broken. Then again, she had never believed in ghosts herself and, if what Jesse had told her was true, Jesse had now spent four days living through nights like last night but with no one, absolutely no one, who would listen to what was going on.

Suzanne had been so furious with Brian that she had been prepared to hate him. Now she had to reevaluate. What she was seeing was a man who was confused and disbelieving but who obviously cared very much for the frail woman who was barely recognizable in her current state.

After Brian left, his arm supporting Jesse as they walked slowly down the side walk, Suzanne poured a cup of tea and took a chair facing Deidra's ring, where it sat in the middle of the kitchen table. She studied it for a long time, hesitant to touch it now that she firmly believed Deidra lived there.

"Deidra, we need to talk," she said. It felt stupid to address the ring but she pushed her doubts away and continued. "You really have to go to wherever ghosts go and leave Jesse alone. You're hurting her."

Nothing. In the light of day Suzanne had already started doubting herself; doubting that what had happened the night before had been a visit from Deidra rather than some wild dream brought on by Jesse's stories. Then she thought of Jesse's

139

exhaustion and drunken depression and continued. If Deidra was here—was wreaking havoc—it had to stop.

"Deidra, don't ignore me." Suzanne waited for something, anything, but like before, she didn't seem to have a connection with Deidra. There was no response. "God damn it, Deidra! Aren't you supposed to 'cross over' or whatever the hell they call it? You need a fucking light?"

Still nothing. Suzanne picked up the ring and studied it. As nice as it was it didn't look like anything abnormal. It certainly didn't look like a ghost was in it. She didn't feel any sharp sting of cold, there wasn't any sudden wind blowing the curtains off the window or slamming drawers. There was nothing.

With a yawn, Suzanne put the ring back down and carried her cup of tea out to the porch. God she was tired, but she couldn't face sleep. Surreal as it had been, part of her knew last night's experience hadn't been a dream. If the crazies were catchy, she was catching them. She wondered if she could really help Jesse if she lost her objectivity, and doubted it. Two women screaming in the middle of the night wouldn't improve the situation at all.

Jesse and Brian picked an outside table at the Summerhouse Grill. The white wrought-iron table and chairs sitting in the middle of the garden gave a feeling of being in another world, separate from death and anger and worry. Light green buds covered the trees, announcing spring's late but welcome arrival. In the flower beds, surrounded by a white picket fence, fresh herbs were already lush and fragrant. Brian could actually see Jesse relax. He ordered coffee for both of them and had the waitress bring wine glasses and uncork the bottle. With relief, he saw Jesse cover the top of her glass with her hand, indicating she didn't want any wine. He certainly did, though. He hadn't smoked in years but now found himself desperately wanting a cigarette, too. It had been a hard week and an even harder day.

Even though the sun was warm, Jesse shivered. Brian saw it and took off his suit coat to drape it around her shoulders. She surprised him by catching his hand and placing a soft kiss on it. Then she held it to her cheek for a moment before letting him go.

"I've missed you," Jesse said with a tired smile. "I shouldn't have sent you away. Who knew I needed you this much?"

"And I should have stayed," Brian agreed. "I'm sorry, Jesse. Whatever happened, I should have been there to see you through."

"What happened was I saw Deidra's ghost, not once but a couple of times, and she insists on breaking things."

Brian felt his back go ridged. "Jesse, we can't go there. I believe you're having a hard time. I believe you think you saw something. I believe a bottle of whiskey will conjure up all kinds of visions. I just don't believe Deidra is visiting you and throwing stuff around your room."

"And I believe that if you insist on dismissing what I'm saying we are going to continue to have problems. You can't help me if you don't believe me." The soft Jesse was gone and Brian knew he'd made a mistake. She pushed her chair back from the table and would have left if he hadn't grabbed her hand.

"Cut me some slack, Jesse. You know I'm a hard facts kind of guy. I don't believe in anything I can't see or prove. That being said, I do believe in you and because you say these things are happening I believe they are. I am just struggling with the idea that Deidra is doing them."

"You wouldn't believe in the second coming if Jesus tapped you on the shoulder and told you his name," she snapped, her voice dripping sarcasm, "but that wouldn't mean it hadn't happened." To his relief she sat back down and picked up the menu. "So, how was your meeting?" Her voice was cold and controlled.

"I have no idea." *I was too worried about you to concentrate*, he thought, but didn't say it. Damn, the last thing Jesse needed was for him to blame her for the botched deal. And maybe it wasn't botched. He was telling the truth when he said he didn't know.

Jesse's slender finger ran down items on the menu and he couldn't help but notice the chipped polish, the nearly transparent skin. Jesse, always thin, appeared to have lost pounds over the past few days. "Do you think we could eat? I'm starving," he said. He knew that Jesse would do it for him even if she wouldn't do it for herself.

They started with a thick bouillabaisse followed by the chipotle brisket. With each bite, Jesse brightened, color returning to her face. When they ordered chocolate-cinnamon buttermilk cake for dessert, Jesse spread her hands and laughed at herself. "Gee, you would think I was hungry or something. I must be ten pounds heavier than when

143

we walked in. Now, let's talk about this endowment that is driving you crazy."

Just as Suzanne's questions about tax breaks had absorbed Jesse in federal loopholes, Brian's breakdown of the endowment issues caught her full attention. Brian marveled again at how much information Jesse stored in her head and how effectively she applied it. How could someone so logical be blown to pieces by what she claimed was a "ghost"?

Suzanne found them that way—leaning toward each other over coffee cups, talking financial strategy and management. She stood at the garden gate for a few minutes, hating to interrupt. This was what drew them to each other, she realized, this passion for putting puzzles together and making things work. They fed on concrete solutions. Now that she knew about Jesse's desperate attempt to flee from the supernatural, it made all the sense in the world; Jesse escaped the unbelievable by drowning herself in perfectly understandable facts. Suzanne was aware that her own appearance was going to draw Jesse back into the other world, and regretted it, but it was unavoidable.

"Is anyone going to offer me some of that lovely wine?" Suzanne quipped as she took a seat at the table. She noticed with satisfaction that the bottle had hardly been touched, and that Jesse's glass was still clean. *So Brian is the antidote*, she thought, and felt proud of having forced his hand.

Brian looked around for the waitress, and Suzanne was struck at how different he looked now. His carefully arranged hair had been messed by the wind and flopped in curls over his forehead. The stiff white shirt was unbuttoned at the neck; the perfectly pressed cuffs were now rolled to the elbows. When he looked at Jesse, a boyish grin changed his face from country-club aloof to college-jock flirt, and even Suzanne could see what kept Jesse mesmerized. He needed Jesse as much as Jesse needed him; he drove away her ghosts and she drove away his deadly seriousness.

"Tell me about yourself," Brian invited. "Were you part of the college orgy scene or did you come along at some other point?"

Suzanne had to laugh at the undisguised question. "If you're asking me if Jesse and I were ever …intimate…" she raised her eyebrows suggestively and paused just long enough to see Brian's eyes start to calculate her as competition, "no. I have always been what you see now and Jesse, in case you didn't notice, likes guys. If you remember correctly, I'm not one."

His laugh was infectious. Jesse looked from one to the other, not getting the joke. "She flashed me," Brian said, "I thought she might be a guy with a very unusual name. You have heard of "A Boy Named Sue", haven't you?"

It took a minute but when Jesse caught on she laughed along with them. "I have to assume I was in a drunken haze at the time?"

"You were indeed, my sweet," Suzanne replied, "and to save you from yourself I think I should finish this nice wine before you get at it."

"Not on your life. We all walked here; we'll stagger home together." A shadow slipped across Jesse's face. "We are going home together, right?" she asked and Suzanne could see fear creep back into Jesse's eyes.

"We are," Brian assured her. "If Deidra is going to come visiting she'll have to visit all of us."

Brian and Suzanne exchanged concerned glances as Jesse filled her glass, but neither of them was prepared to tell Jesse not to drink. "To friends—where would we be without them?" Jesse saluted.

"Cheers," Suzanne agreed. They raised their glasses together and drank, with Jesse's eyes full of relief, Suzanne's with reluctance and Brian's with a lightness that was proof he still didn't believe in ghosts.

Deidra didn't even notice. She had other things to do. This time she would choose where she went and what she did. She hoped—was almost sure—it only took focus.

CHAPTER 15

That night, when it was still cold north of Route 80 and warm to the south, fog rolled across Route 81 in the Poconos and nearly blocked all vision. Only a few people were on the Martz Trailways bus that finally pulled into Scranton at two o'clock in the morning from New York City—a full thirty minutes late. Tired and stiff, the driver breathed a sigh of relief and called out, "Last stop Scranton. Scranton. Please check the overhead racks. You may collect your luggage at the side of the bus. Last stop—Scranton."

Tony Peters was seriously considering putting in a request for a day run. Since that girl had been found dead on the bus he got a shiver every time he had to make a final inspection. He was still having nightmares about it—woke up screaming and scaring the shit out of his wife. He had overheard his son telling a friend, "Dad seriously freaks me out, man."

Tired passengers, mostly college students, roused themselves and grabbed backpacks. He counted them as they disembarked. All were accounted for.

Tony followed them down the steps and pulled suit cases out of the baggage compartment. He thought about using the terminal bathroom before the final bus check but decided five minutes more or less wasn't going to make a difference, and he wouldn't have to come back. He never used the toilet on the bus. It was too small and, by the end of the night, just too disgusting.

This night the fog that created wispy circles around the lights seeped up the stairs and into the open bus door, making everything dreamlike. Tony mounted the steps with a shiver, eager to finish. He walked the length of the bus, removing empty bottles, scattered newspapers, left-over food and chewed gum. People were pigs

Shit. Half way down the bus he could see a figure in an aisle seat. He knew he'd just checked and it was empty. His heart started beating so hard he could feel it trying to break through his chest wall. *Get a grip; some homeless guy*, he told himself.

"Vacate the bus, please," he said in his sternest, most professional voice. "End of the line. Let's go."

Now that he was closer he could see an arm hanging into the aisle. Long fingers brushed the floor. Black hair showed above the seat, a long curl actually hanging over the back. Tony's bladder pushed against his belt, urgent and demanding. His stomach lurched into his lung space, stealing his breath away.

"Excuse me, Miss—er—Ms.," *What the hell was the right thing? These days you couldn't tell; could be a guy for that matter.* "You have to get off the bus now or I'll call the police," he demanded and reached out to shake the person's arm.

His hand passed through empty air. The seat was empty. The whole bus was empty. *I should have used the bathroom*, he thought, and wet his pants.

Deidra nearly laughed herself sick.

CHAPTER 16

Suzanne escaped to the third floor as quickly as she could, desperately in need of a good sleep after the night in Jesse's reading chair. When she couldn't stop yawning, she excused herself, but not before glaring at Brian. "Don't leave her alone."

"I won't," Brian reassured her. Even then Suzanne wasn't convinced, and she stared at him until he waved her away. "Seriously, I'm not going anywhere. Get some sleep."

Half way up the stairs, Suzanne stopped and peered anxiously into the shadows above her. *I'll never be the same*, she thought. The third floor, which had seemed charmingly inviting before, now felt ominous. "If you're up here, Deidra, leave me the hell alone," she ordered.

Brian, standing at the bottom of the stairs, heard her and frowned. Even after being told about the lights, the wind, the computer and what Suzanne referred to as "the kidnapping," he found himself discrediting the story of the night before. He was sure a psychiatrist would have a list of reasons two otherwise logical, intelligent women would have mutual hysterics upon losing a friend. There could have been a storm that moved the pictures, and Jesse was probably sleepwalking, reliving moments in Deidra's play. God knows Jesse had been drinking enough to hallucinate and, since Suzanne was her friend from college, it only made sense that she had been drinking, too, didn't it?

You're being self-righteous, an inner voice warned him, but he shook it off. The alternative—that Deidra was actually in the room, inside of Jesse—was too much to buy into. Then again, Suzanne seemed so rational, so totally concrete that he couldn't imagine her getting crazy, either. But they had just met; what did he know?

"Are you really staying? You don't have to." Jesse's voice surprised him. She had come up behind him as he was watching Suzanne go up the stairs. She motioned for him to follow her out onto the porch and then said softly, obviously not wanting Suzanne to hear them talking. "Suzanne thinks I'm weaker than I really am."

"Maybe, Jesse, but you seem pretty beat up to me." It wasn't what he wanted to say. He wanted to say *I want to stay, please.* But the words got somewhere between his lips and his pride. She had seemed so glad to see him—so happy. What had happened?

"I don't know what's harder—knowing that Deidra comes to visit or knowing that you don't believe me."

"Jesse—," Brian winced as he saw the hurt in her eyes and the shadow of exhaustion on her face. "I believe you believe. Isn't that enough?"

A flush of red crept up Jesse's neck and brightened her face. "No." She turned away from him. "It was awfully nice of you to drop by. I'll tell Suzanne in the morning that you simply left early."

Jesse's rejection hit him like a blow. He felt a tightening band around his heart. He closed his eyes and took in a slow breath before letting himself speak. "I left you before when you asked me to stay and have regretted it ever since. Then you made me leave the funeral without you and I got a desperate call from

Suzanne that I had to come over right away because you needed me. I thought you were with another man and came anyway ...."

"If that's the only reason you're here then you'll feel better if I tell you I don't need you anymore," Jesse snapped.

Brian was puffed up one moment, his hands on his hips, his lips thin and angry and the next Jesse saw him deflate. He bowed his head and let his breath out slowly. His voice softened. "Please let me stay," he said. "I just want to be here with you."

Jesse was taken by surprise and then gave way to a rush of relief. Her bluster was that—just bluster. Another night alone was more than she could bear. She knew she would wind up sleeping on the window seat in Suzanne's room rather than spend one more night waiting for Deidra to show up and do God-knows-what in the wee hours of the morning. But she couldn't forget how she had begged—yes, begged!—him to stay the night Deidra died and the next night and she, too, had pride. Somehow Brian staying because she was a basket-case wasn't enough. Staying because he wanted to be with her was exactly what she needed. She stepped into his arms and rested her head against his chest. Until just now, this minute, she hadn't realized how much she had been missing him even while she was angry and hurt.

"Okay?" he asked.

"Okay," she said.

They sat on the porch, Jesse curled into the corner of the couch, her knees drawn up under her chin and Brian sitting near her, straight and still. Night crawled up the hill from Berry Street until everything around them was pitch-black. As if an agreement had been reached beforehand, neither of them spoke. Finally, Brian heard a soft intake of breath and Jesse began to talk.

"I should tell you some things that I told Suzanne—things that only Deidra knew about me."

"There's no need." Brian wasn't sure what he was about to hear but he didn't want any more stories of sex and drugs and missing underwear.

"There is a need. You see, I'm not just crazy enough to see Deidra's ghost. I've been crazy enough to see ghosts for a long, long time." And she told him about the ghosts on Berry Street: the little girl who was always hiding behind the church, the man hanging from a branch in front of one of the houses. She told him about her determination to stop seeing them and her success in blocking; about her mother passing this gift to her. And she told him why she stopped taking pictures.

"So, you see," she finally said, "if you don't believe me about Deidra, there is a great deal you'll never believe about me in general and nothing, absolutely nothing can go any further with us."

The silence was deafening. She kept herself away from Brian; kept herself curled in a ball there on the end of the couch. So much depended on his reaction.

"You stopped taking pictures because of these "orbs"?

"I did."

"And you only catch them on digital cameras, not old fashioned, manual ones."

"Yes."

"And you're first love is photography?"

"It was."

Brian was silent for a long time. "It seems to me that the answer, if you want to continue, is to only use manual cameras, or," he raised his eyebrows in a question, "you can probably make a lot of money taking ghost pictures. People love that stuff."

Jesse looked up hopefully only to see that Brian was grinning at her, expecting her to laugh. Her heart sank as she realized he hadn't taken anything she had said seriously. "But you don't believe me." Her voice was low and sad.

He couldn't see her face. He only knew that the further she drew away, the closer he wanted to get. The truth in her stories—or at least her own conviction that they were true—was too clear to dismiss. And what made something true anyway? His perception? Hers? Here in the dark, with Berry Street below them, it was easy to believe there were ghosts. It wasn't easy to believe that Jesse could see them. Brian had spent his entire life dealing with cold hard facts and in Jesse he had thought he'd found someone who was like him; absolutely logical.

"Do you think you would have seen ghosts if your mother hadn't told you that you could?" It was the wrong thing to ask. He could tell instantly by the way Jesse curled up even tighter; moved further away from him if that was even possible. For a moment, he wondered if the arm of the wicker couch was going to be strong enough to hold with her pushing so hard against it.

"First of all, I told her about me first and then she confessed about herself to make me feel better. Second, it's all of me or none of me, Brian. I've spent years trying to forget and deny and refuse what I see. This thing with Deidra scares me, but it also proves that I can't ignore the truth anymore about who and what I am. If I don't accept that I can see and hear Deidra then I have to accept that I'm out of my fucking mind, and that will drive me over the edge."

Brian measured his words carefully and spoke slowly, like a patient parent addressing an upset child, "Maybe if you would just accept that Deidra is dead you could get past this. You do know the stages of grief: denial and isolation, anger, bargaining, depression, acceptance. You isolated yourself from me and ..." He didn't get to finish.

Jesse was on her feet and back inside, the door slamming closed behind her, before Brian could finish his statement or even stand up to follow. He heard the lock turn in the old-fashioned dead bolt and knew she had shut him out. He shook the handle, When it didn't budge, he knocked, gently at first and then more urgently. God, he was an idiot. "Jesse! Come on! I'm sorry!" But she didn't open the door. "It takes some time to adjust, you know!" Frustration raised his voice. He stepped back into the yard and clenched his fists. "Let me in!" he yelled, his voice loud enough so she had to hear him wherever she was inside.

The window on the third floor opened, and Suzanne's head appeared, her expression disdainful. "Hey, you! You're waking up the dead! Maybe instead of telling you to stay I should have told you to leave before you could be an ass."

"Just let me in. She locked the door."

Suzanne wasn't sure what the best course to follow really was, but she did remember how Jesse had looked at Brian earlier; how the two of them had touched each other. With a sigh, she disappeared from the window and reappeared at the door in silk boxers and a tank top. "Just try not to be too much of a jerk," she said curtly and walked away, leaving the door open behind her.

Jesse could hear the exchange between Suzanne and Brian. She was pretty sure the entire neighborhood could. Suzanne's, "You're waking up the dead," had made her smile, and suddenly she could see the whole conversation with Brian in a different light. She'd gotten mad at him for not believing in ghosts when, truthfully, almost no one believed in such things. She had sent him away and he hadn't gone. She envisioned him, CEO of the Community

Foundation, golf club board member, Mr. Cool-Calm-and-Collected Brian Carpenter, standing in her yard in the middle of the night yelling and pounding on the door. As quickly as anger had made her walk away, appreciation that he actually still wanted to be there made her happy. The cops and any local reporters would have had a field day if a neighbor had called in a disturbance.

Brian approached Jesse's room hesitantly; afraid of what she would say when she realized he was still there. What he didn't expect was to find Jesse, stripped down to a silk bra and matching panties, laughing at him. "It's just too melodramatic, isn't it?" she gasped and laughed so hard tears ran down her cheeks, "Brian, you are so out of your element."

She looked at his bewildered face, the blond curls sticking straight up where he had been running his fingers through them, the perfect cotton shirt which was now half untucked and wrinkled and the wary look in his always confident eyes, and loved him. "Ghosts and goblins and witches; oh my!" she chanted and moved from laughter to giggles to a tired smile.

"Can we drop this whole thing?" he asked. "I just want to stay and go to bed and deal with it tomorrow." He was grateful when she nodded and then surprised him even more by walking across to him and hugging him tight.

"Yes, we can," she sighed against his chest.

Brian buried his face in her hair, marveling for the millionth time at its softness. "You really could drive me nuts, you know," he said softly.

"I know."

"And I can't just start believing in ghosts, even if you do," he said, slipping his arm around her waist, his hand spread across the bare skin of her back.

"I know."

"Okay then. But I will stop trying to change you or prove you wrong, okay?" He tipped her head back with his free hand and looked into her eyes, "because we should be together, right?"

"Right." A smile played at the corner of her mouth. "However, if you don't want to see a ghost I suggest we turn off the computer, close the window and leave the ring in the kitchen."

She was wrong. Brian and Jesse fell asleep spooned together. His strong hands had run repeatedly down her back, her arms, her legs and worked out the tightly strung muscles he found there. When Jesse had fallen asleep, Brian had stayed awake, listening to the silence around them and watching the darkness of the room.

A light woke Brian up, and he struggled to remember where he was and recognize what was happening. The computer—which he had carefully turned off and checked before getting into bed—was on, its screen flashing images faster than he could identify them. He sat up to shut it off again when a crash next to him shocked him into full consciousness. The dresser drawer opened and slammed, opened and slammed. Soon, all of the drawers were opening and closing in a constant bang. *Dreaming*, he thought. *It's just a dream.*

Perspiration slid down his face. He could feel it sting his eyes and taste its salt on his lips, but he couldn't move. Wind swept across his chest. He glanced at the window, and a groan escaped him as he saw it through the computer-generated strobing lights, still closed and locked. In the wind there was sound, a low whining at first, escalating into a howl, and in the howl he could hear words—not enough to understand, but words just the same.

Beside him, Jesse cried out in her sleep and grabbed the covers, buried her head and shivered. Her body trembled lightly at first and then shook all over.

When she started flailing, he pulled her closer to his chest. She was cold—ice cold. Her eyes opened, vacant and staring. And then, to his horror, she smiled.

"Hello, Brian." Her voice was low, husky—not Jesse's voice. He leaned his body away from her, trying to escape, but she held on to his arm and dragged herself closer, that horrifying grin pasted on her face in something worse than any Halloween mask he'd ever seen.

"Jesus," he gasped.

Jesse laughed. "Not quite, but thank you for the compliment." The tip of her tongue flicked in and out and at his sharp intake of breath she threw back her head and laughed in that chilling, non-Jesse laugh. She ran her hand between his legs and he felt his genitals curl up inside him. "Not glad to see me, I guess," Deidra's voice laughed.

"Jesse, wake up. You're dreaming!" he said sharply. He shook her gently. "Come on, Jesse. Wake up."

Jesse pulled him even closer and ran her tongue up his torso, from his navel to his Adam's apple. "Jesus fuckin' Christ!" he gasped and Jesse laughed. The laughter didn't stop with her but picked up in the wind swirling around them. The speakers on

163

the computer joined in the chorus. Brian threw his hands over his ears, but it went on and on. The computer screen strobed wildly.

Brian rolled off of the bed and hit his head against a dresser drawer that continued to slam in and out. The laughter grew around him, a tunnel of nightmare. "No such thing as ghosts," Jesse giggled and followed him.

She slipped from the bed and danced, her arms extended from her sides, her head thrown back, her hair flying around her. One by one, she slipped the straps of her bra off her shoulders until her breasts were almost entirely exposed. In a seductive sashay, she danced toward Brian, leaned over and held herself out to him. "Just touch me now," Deidra whispered, her voice throaty and demanding. "Touch me—fuck me—I want to feel again."

Brian let out a guttural cry and pushed her away, then tried to catch her as she tripped into the reading chair and fell. "Jesse!" He pulled her up, wrapped her in his arms and held on as the wind swirled around them and the computer continued its frenzied light show. Jesse trembled in his arms. "It'll be alright, Jesse. Just wake up. Wake up!"

He wanted to shake her. He wanted to pick her up and run with her, but to where? Movie scenes flashed through his head of hitting hysterical people to bring them to their senses, of holding up Bibles and crosses and praying away ghosts. Instead, he held the still flailing Jesse tighter and waited. It had to stop, didn't it? If it would just stop, he'd believe anything she said. Anything.

And then, thank God, he heard Suzanne's voice, loud and commanding, order, "Deidra Shay, stop being a bitch—get away from them!" Silence echoed in the room so suddenly he couldn't fathom at first that it was over.

The wind stopped. The drawers froze in various stages of open and closed. Jesse went limp in his arms. All that was left was the computer screen. It froze, leaving one message repeated line after line, "Go home. Go home. Go home."

Brian collapsed to the floor, cradling Jesse in his arms as she cried, crying with her. Suzanne knelt next to them, and Brian slipped his arm around her. She put her arms around both Jesse and Brian, and they huddled together, survivors of a war. Brian rocked them all back and forth, back and forth. There were a million things he wanted to say to Suzanne, but all that came out was, "Thank you. Thank you. Thank you."

Brian was a believer.

CHAPTER 17

At five o'clock, Brian woke up to the sun shining in his eyes. The porch where he and Jesse had finished out the night was damp with dew, and his neck hurt. He carefully eased away from a sleeping Jesse and slipped off the wicker couch. It had certainly never been intended for sleeping.

He kissed Jesse and tucked a blanket more securely around her. She didn't even move. Carefully he kissed her forehead, then her lips. If he hurried he'd be back before she even knew he was gone. He had to get clothes and make a phone call to the office.

Memories of the night before flooded over him, creating a worry line in his forehead. God, he couldn't believe he'd left Jesse to deal with those visitations on her own.

Things might have gone as planned, but they didn't. His cell phone went off at seven, just as he threw a suitcase into the back seat of his car.

"Brian? Robert Brant here. My board has decided the Community Foundation is the right place to handle an endowment. How soon can we meet?"

It took Brian a few seconds to remember exactly who Robert Brant was. Yesterday seemed like years ago. He just wanted to call off work and get back to Jesse before she woke up. His mind did a dizzying run through his memory banks. *Capitol Gas and Oil—the library! Shit!*

"Mr. Brant, I'm so glad you've decided to entrust the Community Foundation with this important endowment. I'll be happy to meet with you any time tomorrow to finish …"

"Today would be better for us, Mr. Carpenter," the voice interrupted. "Surely you understand. I have the papers here that you prepared. It's just a question of our signatures. You do have a notary?"

Brian forced himself to focus. "Yes. Yes, of course we do." *For the library*, he thought. *She'll understand.* "What time would work for you?"

"I'm at your office now, Brian. Surely you're on your way at this late hour?"

Seven in the morning late? For God's sake, how early did this guy think offices opened? But he knew, actually. When people talk about millions they pretty much figure offices open whenever they say so—and they do. "Certainly," Brian assured him. "I'm actually in my car and on my way." He didn't add that he was dressed in a golf shirt instead of a dress shirt; that he was wearing khakis instead of a suit. Let Mr. 24-hour-a-day-Brant think whatever he wanted. Brian Carpenter was going to meet him in a very nice business-casual kind of style. Hopefully fashion wasn't the deciding point. "I'd love to buy you coffee," he ventured.

"That's okay, your office will do fine. I have a breakfast meeting when we're done. I would like to be able to present them with signed contracts—just to head off any discussion of some other, more appropriate place for the funds—right?"

"Of course," Brian agreed automatically. But there's a ghost who might fuck up the love of my life if I do this, he wanted to say, and knew he couldn't. He thought thankfully of Suzanne and decided Jesse would be safe for another half hour or so.

He was thinking a million things, actually, which is why he didn't see the truck marked Capitol Gas and

Oil run through the yellow light; he put on his brakes, but not soon enough. His Volkswagen Jetta was no match for the tanker. "Jesse," he thought, and lost consciousness. The roses that he had purchased while getting gas at the Pump 'n Pantry hit the dashboard and then the floor, exploding in a crimson wet mess all over the leather seats.

"He's gone," Jesse said. She took another sip of hot spiced tea and huddled in the chair by the kitchen table. "He's gone and not coming back."

"He pissed himself and needed a change of clothes," Suzanne stated matter-of-factly, but Jesse just shook her head and spun the ring around and around in her hand.

"I don't know why I keep dancing," Jesse mused. "Do you think I really did those things to Brian? Said those things? I can't even remember doing any of it."

Suzanne just shook her head. "We all know you can't dance, Sweetheart. Deidra is doing it. Honest-to-god possession. Isn't that wild? Although it's too bad you can't remember some of it because your dancing is getting much better, and if it was you instead of

Deidra saying those things to Brian ...oo-la-la...maybe you should let Deidra keep giving you lessons."

Jesse gave Suzanne a dirty look but just got a laugh in response. "Come on, Chickie. If you don't laugh you're going to cry, and you've done enough of that."

"I didn't want to let her go," Jesse said quietly. "And now, look what I've done."

Suzanne grabbed the ring from Jesse and threw it toward the garbage. "Look what she's done." She glared at Jesse, her dark, fine brows pulling close together. "Deidra did this. She hated Brian, didn't want him with you, and she did this, Jesse, not you."

Jesse shook her head slowly back and forth and met Suzanne's gaze. "I held on to her. I called her. I couldn't stand to live without her, and see? This is what happened."

"So what are you going to do next?" Suzanne waited not so patiently for Jesse to say what was on her mind. It was so, so plain that Jesse was thinking something she wasn't telling.

"I'm going to New York," Jesse said and got up and headed to her bedroom. "I'm turning my business over to my manager and going to New York."

"What good will that do? Deidra haunts you so you go to where she's bound to be stronger? Are you crazy? She ordered Brian to go home and now that's what he's done, because he thinks it's what's best for you. You're throwing your life away for her? What the fuck?" Suzanne was way past the point of soft talking. If she could, she would kill Deidra again after all of the pain Deidra had caused. "I saw how you looked at Brian. You belong here—with him!"

Jesse turned back to Suzanne, slowly. "She wasn't telling Brian to go home."

"Really? And just what do you think 'go home' means?"

"She wants to go home, Suzanne, and home is New York."

"And what about Brian?"

"I can't do anything about Brian until I get things settled." Jesse's face softened. She took a deep breath and let it out slowly, her head bending to her chest as if it were just too heavy to hold up anymore. "Even then … oh, Suzanne, I wish …" Her voice trailed off, but that was okay. Suzanne knew what she meant. She knew Jesse loved, truly loved Brian. That was the next sorrow to deal with.

Suzanne thought about the "Go home" Deidra had plastered across the computer screen. She opened her mouth to argue with Jesse and stopped. It made sense. Deidra had been some little misfit, searching for a home. And in New York she was a star, was loved and was engaged to be married. Suzanne threw her hands up in surrender. "You knew her better than anyone else did. If you say she wants to go home, I'll go with you."

It was Jesse's turn to be surprised. "Don't you have things you need to do? A girlfriend waiting or something? Some new advertisement that has deadlines? I can do this myself."

"No," Suzanne snapped angrily. "I came here to fix things, and I'm going to do that as long as you need me to. Good Lord, Jesse. When are you going to stop internalizing?"

Jesse couldn't help but laugh. "I don't think I've been internalizing for a couple of days now. I'm so honest it makes my stomach hurt—no lies, no secrets, no nothing."

"Okay, then. Let's finish this together so I can be the good guy. I've always wanted to be a cowboy with a white hat," Suzanne threw her a wicked grin. "Us queer folks don't get the chance to live out our fantasies all that often."

"Marshal Dillon, I presume?"

"I guess you aren't Miss Kitty?"

"You wish," Jesse couldn't believe how easily Suzanne could make her smile, but she was grateful. "So put on your white hat, Cowboy. We're taking Deidra home as soon as I can pack a bag. And pick up that ring—you missed the garbage."

Deidra didn't hear their conversation. She was on a roll. Her power was growing, and there were places to go and things to do. She had learned a lot about controlling where she went and what she did. She had loved finally making that cold, remote, judgmental Brian pay, and if he stayed away from Jesse for the rest of his life that was just fine with her.

There was a moment when she had looked at Jesse, weak and crying after Deidra had taken over her body for a while, and felt regret. She knew she was using Jesse, and she could see it was doing damage.

Rage filled Deidra—rage at the unfairness of things. Rage at life being taken from her. Rage that she couldn't feel, really feel. She had worked her way into Jesse's body just to have that experience again;

just to be held and comforted. But Brian had ruined it. Brian had rejected her and then she'd had way too much fun scaring the shit out of him. *But look what you did to Jesse*, a little voice in her heart scolded.

"Serves her right for being with that dick-wad anyway!" she screamed back. She wasn't right and she knew it. For a moment, real fear flooded through her—fear of who or what she was becoming. Just one more thing, Jesse, and then I want to go home. Deidra trusted Jesse. Jesse would understand. Jesse was the only one who would help her make sense of this mess.

But she had learned some things through her encounter with Brian. She could do things, all kinds of things, and she had something important to do.

Sammy Allen loosened his tie, rolled up his sleeves, lounged back comfortably behind the desk and waited. He had been teaching for twelve years and enjoyed it more every day. Over the years, Mr. Sammy Allen had learned that if you pay attention to a little geek she'll give you, well, anything. His tutoring session with Jenny wasn't for another hour, which was okay because Sammy had other things to think about.

The newspaper spread across his desk was open to the entertainment section, and there, taking up a full quarter of the page, was a picture of Deidra Shay. This wasn't the Deidra Shay he had known in the early part of his career, but the new improved version, about seventy-five pounds lighter and definitely a woman who made other women fade in comparison.

He still remembered the dark, sullen girl who had claimed a seat in the back of his classroom and made him look stupid by knowing more than he did. He had never seen her with a book, never seen her pay attention in class for that matter, but she had skated through AP Chemistry with straight hundreds and even had the audacity to contradict him when she did bother to pick her head up off the desk during a lecture.

But she was lonely and had the same Cinderella dreams as any girl. That night, he had stayed late to help her with a particularly difficult lab experiment. Their heads were close together, bent over the microscope, and their hands touched frequently as they adjusted dials, made notes, took up the same space. All the while he could see right down the neck of that crazy black dress thing, and no matter how far he looked there didn't seem to be an end to the cleavage.

Maybe he should write a little memoir piece about their great love affair. She couldn't exactly deny it from the grave, could she? She couldn't tell anyone that she had still been a student and that halfway through she had cried, sobbing as she finished him off. She couldn't tell anyone that her breakdown had made him so excited he had come long before he really wanted to; just couldn't hold back anymore. She couldn't say she had fled from the room after throwing everything on his desk to the floor and even some at his head.

"You do have to be in class for the rest of the year to get that A," he had told her as he zipped his pants, and she had shown up every day. She had real guts, that girl. Sammy closed his eyes to get a clearer picture of his memory. A cold breeze across the back of his neck surprised him into opening them again. There, in the back row where she had always been, sat Deidra Shay—not the fat geeky giant Deidra, but the full-blown fantasy Deidra pictured in the newspaper.

Something was wrong with the lights in the room. They dimmed until he had to squint to see her there, watching him from shadows. Fear ran a cold finger up his spine and froze his lungs. Unbelievably, she smiled.

They stared at each other for what seemed like hours but could only have been seconds, and then Deidra crooked her finger and beckoned him forward. He couldn't move, but she could. Suddenly she was in the front row.

He could see that the black dress was really a slip, and a skimpy one at that. Through the thin fabric, erect nipples could be seen straining forward. Slowly, Deidra's tongue reached out to moisten her top lip, moved ever so softly back and forth, and then slipped back into her mouth, taking a moment to graze perfectly white teeth. She slipped lower in the desk chair, exposing legs that went on and on, lean thighs that flexed to raise her pelvis a little higher.

Was she flashing him a beaver? She was. Her hips thrust forward just the tiniest bit—just enough to show she was wearing absolutely nothing under the skimpy slip. He was hypnotized as he saw her finger go there, touch in a constant rhythm and slip inside. She shook her head back and closed her eyes, still in motion.

It was more than he could stand. Fear gave way to desire. He'd never fucked a ghost, but this one was obviously inviting him to have the experience of his life. He got up and walked toward her, slowly, carefully, waiting for her to disappear but instead she opened her eyes just the tiniest bit, bit her bottom lip and with her free hand reached for him.

He hardly realized what he was doing as he unzipped his pants, let them fall to the floor and then kicked them aside. He stood in front of her, released his now painful erection from the opening of his boxer shorts and lowered his head toward the deep valley between her breasts.

She pulled the slip away exposing herself totally, reached her hand out to touch him and …

Deidra was well aware of the ice cube temperature of her touch. She had resented it, regretted it, been dismayed by it but never had she been so entirely gratified to have it.

The cold that jolted through Sammy Allen's penis sent it scurrying back into his scrotum, which screamed and climbed up into his stomach and pushed vomit gushing out of his mouth. He watched in horror as Deidra laughed and licked his puke off of her lips. And she pushed harder.

Ice wrapped around Sammy's heart and stopped it cold. His lungs couldn't move in and out. He gasped and fell to his knees and still she squeezed at him, pushed at him.

This pain couldn't go on, could it? Jolts shot up his left arm and into his shoulder. He felt his chest contract. He was imploding, dying, and he screamed. He kept screaming long after Deidra was done laughing, long after Jenny found him and frantically pushed 911 on her cell phone with shaking fingers, long after the paramedics arrived and carried him away on the stretcher. He screamed until the orderlies in the psych ward at Binghamton General Hospital pumped him full of tranquilizers that put him blessedly to sleep.

After the surgery to try and repair the damage he had done ripping at his crotch, Deidra sat next to his bed in recovery and nodded as he struggled through the drug-infused fog to see her and start screaming again.

Deidra smiled. There was justice in the world after all.

CHAPTER 18

Connor pulled himself out of another alcohol and drug-induced coma, struggled to find the phone, and finally gave up. He'd get the message later. He pulled the covers over his head to block the sun shining through the window and went back to sleep.

Since Deidra's death, Connor had spent more and more time hiding in a chemically altered state. Being fully conscious and aware was far too painful. His unruly red curls were bushier, his beard longer and his clothes had started hanging on the body he no longer cared to feed. On days like this he knew he had to snap out of it, but he had no idea how to go about it.

Much later—was it hours? Days?—his doorbell rang. He stumbled out of bed, cursing as he stubbed his toe, wrapped a sheet around himself and threw the door open. He blinked in confusion at the sight of

Bethany standing there holding some kind of dish in front of her.

There was no doubting her beauty. Tall like Deidra, but muscular and whipcord thin from years of dancing, she was breathtaking. Her long straight hair was pulled back in a ponytail, and she looked fresh and innocent in her jeans and denim jacket. But Connor had no problem remembering the way Bethany had stalked him when he was dating Deidra; how Bethany had made it clear over and over again that she wanted everything Deidra had and more, including Deidra's lead in the play and Deidra's man. He doubted that even Bethany knew that her latest efforts to seduce him had little to do with wanting him but rather wanting to be what Deidra had been.

"I'm not in the mood," he said gruffly and tried to close the door.

"Food." Bethany smiled, ignored his glare and pushed past him into the studio apartment. She set the dish down by the stove, washed two bowls and two glasses and set them on the tiny table. "I can't fix much that's wrong with you but I can feed you." Her tone was cheerful and matter-of-fact, without even a hint of flirtation.

"I'm not hungry."

"Yes, you are. Sit."

Connor sat more in response to the sudden dizziness that spun his head around than to Bethany's command, but he could tell by her smile that she thought otherwise. He was surprised when she filled his bowl with what appeared to be honest-to-god homemade chicken noodle soup. His stomach surprised him by growling hungrily at the sight and good smell. For a change, he was honestly grateful for Bethany's intrusion into his little apartment.

"You didn't do this yourself, right? You hardly seem like the cooking type."

"I wasn't born here, you know. I'm from West Virginia, and in West Virginia everybody learns how to cook." Bethany served herself a small scoop of broth without any noodles or meat and sat down across from him.

Connor eyed her nearly empty bowl. "That's all you're having?"

Bethany shrugged. "I'm used to not eating much. It's bad for my career."

Connor's laughter surprised both him and Bethany. She looked up to see him shaking his head and grinning. "Damn fool idea, that one. Deidra knew how to eat and how to drink, and she knew that her hips and chest made men salivate. You're an actress, not a runway model."

"Deidra would have looked better several pounds lighter." Her tone was critical and she blushed as she realized what she had let slip out. "I'm sorry," she said quickly. "Deidra was who she was and I'm who I am."

"But you think you're better, right?" Connor wasn't laughing any more but he didn't seem angry either. "You think that if she can do it you can because you're better—thinner, more disciplined, more serious, right?"

Bethany took little sips of soup and didn't respond or look at him.

"Look at me, Bethany," he said softly. When she didn't respond Connor reached a large hand over and cupped her chin, forcing her to look up. "Deidra had passion. You have training and desire and a great work ethic. But Deidra had passion that made everyone love her, believe her and in your case, disdainful as you may be, want to be her. You'd do better to find yourself."

Bethany's eyes blazed. "I don't want to be Deidra! I would just like to be recognized for who I am, and yes, I am a little bit sick of being compared to her like I'm no one and she's God's gift to men and theatre. Tell me, Connor. What was it about her that you loved so much when you wouldn't give me the time of day?"

There were very few times Connor could remember when Bethany had actually talked to him instead of simply touching, teasing, testing. He decided that maybe this girl, the one in denim and bearing chicken soup was here as a real person. He had spent lots of time in the theatre and behind the camera. His family had been well known both as agents and directors in the New York scene for generations. Maybe she wanted an honest answer. Maybe this wasn't just another come-on. He decided to be honest.

"Deidra wasn't just another hopeful. She had a BFA and was working on her MFA. But the biggest thing was that she wasn't looking for the threatre to give her anything. She just loved it. She was happy as an understudy and happy as a scene hand, if that was all she could do. She wanted to give to the theatre in any way she could. She welcomed every opportunity to throw herself into it and learn something new. You, on the other hand, want the theatre to give something to you."

Bethany rolled her eyes but Connor ignored that and continued. "You want to get something, and that something is what? Recognition? Fame? What? But you seem to think you deserve something automatically, and you resent anyone else being recognized. If you just throw your heart in it without worrying about reimbursement maybe, just maybe, you'll find your place there. It's not a competition."

Bethany stared at her soup for a long time. Finally she stood up and cleared the table as Connor watched her. When everything was washed, she leaned against the sink and spoke quietly. "You're wrong about some things and right about others, Connor. I came here for two reasons—well, three, actually."

"And they are?"

"One, I really have been worried. Talk is that you're always drunk out of your mind and losing weight and I remember my Grandma Oaks saying the body and heart both need chicken soup when sick."

Connor held up his hand as if to silence her but Bethany ignored it.

"Second, I want to ask you to come to the play opening night. I know who you are and who your family is, and I would appreciate your take on my performance. And third, I want a token of Deidra for that night—a good luck charm, so to speak." She saw the angry flush wash across his face and hurried on before he could interrupt. "I know that Deidra and I didn't get along, but as you said, she would give anything and everything for the success of the show and—it's hard to explain—I am thinking about the Deidra kick, and—" her voice trailed off.

"And? What is it that you want of Deidra's?" Connor's voice was hard. He didn't know what was coming but he knew he wasn't going to like it. The soup he had enjoyed was now turning his stomach.

"Well, I don't want the actual item, but I would like to know where to get—Connor, I want to get a pair of those light-up panties and I know you can direct me to the right place. I mean, I wouldn't want hers of course, but a pair of my own? The audience expects that, you know."

"That isn't part of the play, Bethany. That's Deidra having fun at curtain calls."

"She made it a part of the play and I think …"

"It's hers and hers alone. If you're as good as you say, you can come up with something of your own." Connor pushed himself back from the table, not careful of staying modest and not careful to cover his anger and disgust. "I think you should leave now."

Bethany stepped close to him, close enough to brush lightly against his bare chest and torso; close enough to surprise him with a rush of blood to his groin. It made him mad. "Connor—"

"Not one more word." He pulled his robe closed and mentally gave a nod to victims of sexual assault. At some level he felt violated, forced and abused. "You really do want to be her, don't you? Well, on your best day you can't begin to be anything near as good as Deidra at her worst, you got it? And that skinny butt of yours wouldn't look good in panties designed to show off a real woman. I'm going to lose it any second," he grabbed Bethany by the elbow and pulled her toward the door, "so I think you should leave before that happens." He opened the door and shoved her out. "As for me being there, I think I will. I think I'm going to enjoy watching you fail miserably." With that, he slammed the door. Bethany couldn't miss the sound of the dead bolt turning.

Connor dumped the rest of the soup down the trash compactor and threw Bethany's dish in the garbage. He had no intention of returning it and was pretty sure Bethany wouldn't be coming back to ask for it. Angry with himself and with her, he pulled on a pair of boxer shorts and started cleaning up.

One thing Bethany had said stuck with him, and he planned on changing it. People were saying he had fallen apart. Well, he had, but that was going to end. What he had said about Deidra was true: she was about giving rather than getting, and he had been wallowing heavily in the feel-sorry-for-myself swamp, which was definitely a getting thing. He hadn't given any thought to Jesse, Deidra's best friend, or Mary, Deidra's mother. He hadn't checked on the play even though the entire cast had to be worried about how things would go without Deidra carrying the show. It was time to get back to the business of living.

As he washed the last dish, he sensed someone behind him and turned, expecting just for a moment to see Deidra but, of course, no one was there. He headed for the shower and saw a shadow flit across the corner of the hall and turned to look but again, no one was there. "Get a grip," he ordered himself. "It's fatigue, paranoia and loneliness. You should write a country song." The idea made him smile, and he started humming as the warm shower water rolled over his shoulders. A hand touched his back and he whirled around to find even more empty space. "Deidra," he whispered. He knew that touch, but she was gone, wasn't she? She'd never touch him again. Angry with himself, he cut his shower short and got out, pulling on a comfortable sweat shirt and well-worn denims. It was time to take his life back.

The idea that someone was in the apartment kept haunting him. An efficiency doesn't have any place for a person to hide, but he still found himself spinning around, expecting to surprise the intruder. Several times, he thought he felt Deidra touch him; touch his neck, touch his hair, like she used to.

The door buzzer startled him, as did his first thought—Deidra lost her key again. He knew it for the lie it was the second it entered his head, but he couldn't shake the feeling that Deidra was there. It was Bethany's fault, he knew, for bringing up all that stuff—all that talk had messed with him. And now Bethany was probably back to hassle him again. He was suddenly furious.

Connor threw the pillow he had just picked up off the floor and rushed to the door. *No more Mister Nice-Guy,* he thought. He threw the door wide, "I warned you—," he growled and then stopped. For one wild moment it was Deidra standing there—and then it wasn't. His heart lurched into his throat so that he couldn't say a word, just stood there staring.

"Hi, Connor. Hope we didn't catch you at a bad time." He just stared at Jesse and Suzanne and they stared back, looking as confused as he did.

His voice came out in a harsh croak, "What are you doing here?"

"I brought you something," Jesse said.

She held out her hand. Connor stared at the lovely diamond ring he had turned down two times before. This time he accepted it, gently picking it out of her palm as if it were fragile. He curled his fingers around it and held his closed hand against his chest. They stood in silence as Connor closed his eyes and took a slow, uneven breath. His face relaxed and his lips curved in a slow smile. "She knew she was coming home," he whispered.

"I'm sure she did," Jesse assured him. "May we come in?"

Connor opened the door wide and let Jesse, Suzanne and Deidra enter.

CHAPTER 19

Jesse and Suzanne looked around, taking in the small space tastefully furnished in heavy leather furniture and mahogany shelves, table and chairs. Despite the dark furnishings, the studio unit felt spacious and light. A wall of windows opened to the Hudson, and Jesse knew this one room was worth twenty of her house. It didn't matter where or how Connor had come by money; he had more than anyone would have guessed based on his shabby appearance.

For a bachelor pad, it was surprisingly clean, but then Jesse didn't know what it had looked like an hour earlier, before Connor had made himself claim his life back. Suzanne nodded at the recycling bags in the kitchen filled with bottles and raised her eyebrows. "A little self-medicating?"

"Pain killers," Connor acknowledged and Suzanne sighed.

"I wouldn't object to a little pain killer myself," she suggested. Gratefully, Connor grabbed freshly washed glasses and set them on the coffee table with a bottle of unopened Glenfiddich.

"Water and ice on the refrigerator door." He nodded toward the kitchen area. "It's closer and colder than if I put it in bowls and pitchers."

"Not Jack Daniels?" Jesse couldn't help but ask. This was, after all, Deidra's man.

"Only when I'm suicidal," Connor replied. Suzanne and Jesse both noticed that he didn't smile when he said it.

They sat in uncomfortable silence for several minutes, each sipping the Scotch and trying to figure out where to start a conversation. Suddenly everything that had happened in the preceding days seemed too implausible to put into words. But the only thing or person the three of them had in common was Deidra, and the conversation had to open that way. There was nothing else to talk about.

"You brought me the ring for a reason," Connor suggested. "How about telling me what that reason is?"

Suzanne put her hand protectively on Jesse's knee. "Deidra has been getting a little crazy, and Jesse thinks she wants to come home. We think the ring acts as a conduit and Deidra is attached to it somehow."

"You know that sounds crazy, right? And you keep speaking of Deidra in the present tense." Connor's tone was flat. No matter how hard Jesse studied him she couldn't tell what he was thinking.

Suzanne wasn't fazed. If she could get uptight Brian to believe what was happening, she didn't think a free-thinker from the theatre world was going to be too much of a problem. "Don't go testing Jesse before you've heard everything she's got to say. She's been through enough."

And so they told him all of it: the Facebook posts, the wind, the way things got moved around and Deidra's ability to take over Jesse's body. Through it all, Connor kept that blank, non-committal stare until Suzanne wanted to shake him and Jesse simply wanted to leave.

Finally, they were done, ending with Brian's defection that morning. Connor sat silent and still without responding. Just as Jesse and Suzanne exchanged glances, silently agreeing to leave and starting to stand, Connor spoke. "Are you telling me that Deidra can speak through you?" he asked Jesse. "That she can move around as you, dance as you?"

"Yes," Jesse nodded her head. Her sincerity was clear.

"And this isn't an attempt to get me to buy a séance or some stupid thing like that? A rip-off?"

Suzanne was on her feet in a split second, pulling Jesse up with her. "You really are a prick, you know that? We brought you the ring because Deidra says she wants to go home and now she can make your life a living hell and drive you crazy. All right? Good luck with all that."

Jesse wasn't so quick. She remembered Bethany's behavior and was in touch with many of Deidra's New York friends. She held out her hand and very quietly said, "I believe there are other people who would be more interested in having Deidra get in touch with them, maybe dance with them, teach them a few things. How about I give the ring to Bethany? She might appreciate it."

Connor's face flushed. "I just want to know what your motivation is, that's all. Sit down." It was an order but Jesse and Suzanne didn't mind. They were all too aware that their stories were hard to swallow.

"Check her Facebook page," Suzanne said. "We'll wait."

"I don't need to. You guys tell me the ring is the conduit. I don't think so. I think Jesse is, and I want to talk to Deidra."

It took a while for Jesse to understand what Connor was asking for, and when she did he could see her face turn white and her eyes widen. "You want me to let Deidra inside on purpose. You want Deidra through me."

"No!" Suzanne couldn't help herself. "You haven't seen what it does to Jesse. You haven't heard how angry and vulgar Deidra has gotten. It's not like you think. It's a nightmare!"

"It might be different if I'm there;" he said softly, "if Jesse is in control from the beginning."

"I won't allow it," Suzanne stated firmly. "It's downright unhealthy—and what would Brian say?"

"Brian?" Jesse let out a short bark of a laugh. "Let's see," she held up her cell phone, "nope, no calls. Brian has had enough and has taken a powder, alright? No ghosts for Brian. He's had it."

"I don't know what's going on, but I know you're wrong," Suzanne wasn't sure how or why she knew that, but she did. She could picture the look on his face whenever Jesse was near him, the way he had held her, the way Brian and Jesse reached out to each other automatically while in conversation, and Suzanne was absolutely sure that there was an explanation for Brian's sudden absence. It struck her that only forty-eight hours ago she, too, would have assumed the worst, but that had all changed.

Suzanne suddenly yawned and stretched her arms out wide. "I would love to continue this, but I think I need a nap—too many short nights. Can we finish later?"

"You're kidding right?" Jesse gasped. "We're talking about ghost possession and it makes you tired? What's going on?"

"She's avoiding the subject," Connor answered for Suzanne. "She wants time to talk you out of it and she hasn't figured out how to do that yet."

"I see." Jesse gave Suzanne a long, searching once-over. "Maybe I don't need a rest. Maybe I'm not tired."

"No. You're just crazy," Suzanne snapped. "I, on the other hand, need to think. Okay?"

Jesse's face blushed dark enough to make Suzanne start to worry she was having a stroke. "I hardly see where this is your business."

"Really? It seems like it's become my business. I'm not willing to exchange you for Deidra; I'm not willing to lose you." Suzanne covered her eyes and took a deep breath. "Listen—I'm beat. I'll make a deal with you."

"What kind of deal?"

"Don't decide until after the play tonight. I have a hot date and you'll be all on your own. Do whatever you want, but take some time to think. Deal?"

Suzanne was relieved and surprised to see Connor nod thoughtfully. "That makes sense," he said slowly.

Suzanne and Jesse were half way to the hotel before Suzanne realized why Connor had agreed. He would be alone with Jesse/Deidra and Suzanne wouldn't be there to interfere. Worry nagged at her. What exactly did Connor want?

Deidra twitched with impatience. She sat next to Connor and waited for Jesse's reply. She could visit, she could even be seen now and then, but she couldn't feel Connor's touch unless Jesse let her in, and Jesse, in her awake and controlled state, had to make that decision consciously. *One time*, Deidra begged. *Just one time. Please, please, please.* Jesse was the only one who could do it, and Deidra knew that Jesse would do anything for her. But did Jesse know how much this mattered? Did Jesse realize this was for her, Deidra, and not for Connor? And what kind of friend are you to ask for this?

The thought scared Deidra. Was she becoming someone—something—else? She waited. Here was Jesse, able to give Deidra this one thing, and she was refusing. *Selfish bitch*, Deidra thought, and wondered if she meant Jesse or herself.

The Endless Mountains Health System was an out-of-date, under-funded organization that included a clinic and a small hospital. Brian Carpenter was brought into the emergency unit in a semi-conscious state with skull lacerations deep and ugly enough to be indicative of something more underneath. As soon as Brian's eyes opened, he started thrashing against the restraints on the stretcher. The doctor administered enough sedative to prevent additional injury to the spinal cord if any existed, hooked Brian to a monitor for all vitals and sent the ambulance on to Scranton, where a neurologist was waiting. He wondered who Jesse might be. It was the only thing Brian had said in those few moments of consciousness.

"I need to get some bottled water," Suzanne lied and left Jesse at the hotel. As soon as she knew for sure she was out of ear-shot, Suzanne called the Community Foundation. "Mr. Carpenter, please."

"I'm sorry; Mr. Carpenter isn't in right now. Mr. Peters is taking his calls. May I connect you?"

Suzanne sighed, exasperated. "This is highly confidential. I must speak with Mr. Carpenter."

"He'll be out of the office for an undetermined amount of time," the cool, professional voice said. "I assure you Mr. Peters will respect your confidentiality."

"*Personal* and confidential," Suzanne insisted.

"If you have a personal matter to discuss with Mr. Carpenter, perhaps you should try his cell phone," the professional voice replied.

Cell phone. Shit. Suzanne didn't have Brian's cell phone number but Jesse would. So how was she supposed to get it without letting Jesse know what she was up to? And why wasn't he going to be at work? It didn't make sense unless …

Suzanne gasped. Something had happened to him. That had to be it. "Ma'am? Is Brian ill? Is he hurt?"

"I'm not at liberty to discuss Mr. Carpenter's private affairs."

"Okay, just tell me this, and it will be public information so you might as well tell me and save me the bother of calling the local hospitals and police. Has there been an accident?"

Silence answered Suzanne's desperate question. Finally, the voice came back, hesitant and questioning. "Are you a family member?"

"Yes," Suzanne's reply was immediate. "This is his Aunt Suzanne. We had a dinner date and he hasn't shown up."

"Oh dear; I hate to be the one …"

"Just tell me!" Suzanne knew she was yelling but she was also pretty sure that Brian's aunt would be a little upset with this conversation. Her tone might even help. A sudden thought put an edge of hysteria into her voice. "He isn't dead, is he? Is he dead?"

"No, no. I didn't mean to upset you. But you might want to call another family member for more information …" The voice didn't have time to finish. Suzanne had hung up.

Connor wasn't prepared for the lovely woman who emerged from the elevator into the lobby. He had seen Jesse only twice—at the funeral, where she had seemed like a lost, exhausted, tear-swollen child and at his apartment, where she had simply looked like a kid in her jeans and sweat shirt. This Jesse was a different person all together.

She wore the requisite little black dress, offset by high heels and pearls. Her hair hung to her shoulders in soft brown waves, highlighted with strands of gold which caught the light. In make-up and a fitted velvet duster that had to be from the 1930s, she was exquisite, and for the first time Connor saw her for herself. Suddenly he wondered if he could really find Deidra in this woman, or if he even wanted to. Jesse was more than a road to Deidra; she fully and totally took his breath away. He wondered for a second how this Brian guy had ever let her go.

"The theatre is a treat for me. I hope I'm not overdressed," she smiled softly at him.

"New York doesn't have an overdressed." He held out a red rose to her, the one he thought he was buying for Deidra, and watched with pleasure as she blushed.

"You didn't need to, but thank you."

Connor had been relieved when Suzanne had said she had other things to do, but in the taxi cab he missed her contribution to conversation. He had expected Jesse to be more like Deidra—outspoken and runaway talkative—but instead Jesse was quiet, not withdrawn but just quiet. Her eyes followed the city outside the car window, and an occasional smile crossed her face, or a look of sympathy. Connor found himself trying to think of things to say; finally he just gave up and watched. To his surprise, he began to enjoy the silent communication.

"You and Deidra weren't a lot alike, were you?" he observed.

"We were in the ways that mattered."

"Such as?"

Jesse turned her attention to Connor. "You're trying to say she was a lot more interesting, right? It's true. Deidra was fun and I watched."

"That's not true at all." Connor struggled to explain himself, but everything sounded like either a come-on or an insult. "Deidra was ...fire. Fire is very exciting and you expect to get burned but it's worth the adrenalin rush. You know?"

"And I'm not exciting." Connor was afraid Jesse felt put down but a quick glance at her face reassured him.

"You're more like …lovely."

"I'm more like … boring," she said with a smile and went back to staring out the window.

"I've yelled at you, accused you of lying, comforted you and shared your memories of Deidra. Now I've asked you to use your body to give me one more contact with Deidra, and through all of it I've never actually asked you about yourself. That makes me a first-rate jerk, don't you think?"

Jesse took longer to answer than was comfortable. Just as Connor was going to give up entirely she sighed and replied, "I'd pretty much written you off as some kind of Neanderthal, you know. And then you were warm and caring at the hotel, so I put it down to sorrow and let it go. At your apartment, you were suspicious, rude and paranoid but I was willing to let you contact Deidra for her sake, not yours. Now you're downright romantic and seductive. Are you by any chance bi-polar?"

The direct question caught Connor off guard. He stared at her, his mouth open with no words coming out until he let out a roaring, infectious laugh and that surprised a smile from Jesse. A giggle escaped her, and soon she was laughing out loud at their ridiculous situation, their ridiculous plan, their ridiculous actions since knowing each other, and once she started laughing Connor laughed even harder.

Connor finally pulled himself together and gasped, "Oh my god, you are too much. Bi-polar. Whew!" He wiped his eyes. "Well, you might not talk as much as Deidra did but you certainly are direct. That was what you had in common, right? You don't have any self-censoring capability—none of that socially correct awareness."

"Oh, I self-censored myself to death," Jesse disagreed, "but I've given it up lately. Maybe Deidra and I just accepted each other, so self-censoring wasn't necessary."

"No," Connor said.

"No what?

"No, I'm not bi-polar, or at least I've never been diagnosed as such. I'm wildly grief-stricken and out of my mind, hung-over, and naturally suspicious—but not bi-polar. Then again, I'm crazy enough to want to see a ghost, so maybe I am crazy but still, in another time and place you might have even liked me. You might have even said I was charming. 'Oh, Deidra's fiancé is just so very charming,' you might have said. And Deidra and I would have laughed all the way home because she knew that I am, indeed, a jerk. And for that I want to apologize."

"And Deidra loved you because?"

"Because I worshipped the ground she walked on," he said solemnly.

"As did I," Jesse told him, and went back to watching the world pass by the window.

The neurologist at the Community Medical Center in Scranton rushed the accident victim from Montrose into surgery to release the fluid which was rapidly building up on his brain. The paperwork went directly to the nurse's station in the hands of the ambulance driver, who stopped to flirt with the pretty aide he had taken to dinner the week before. The volunteer at the information desk assured Suzanne that no one named Brian Carpenter had been admitted.

Deidra sat happily between Connor and Jesse, thrilled to be going to the theatre; eager to be part of her wonderful play; relieved to be coming home.

CHAPTER 20

Bethany had never been so frustrated in her life. With Deidra gone, she had been so sure that the show would simply go on, as they say; move uptown and go on drawing crowds, go on getting great reviews, go on being the next best thing since Wonder Bread. She was wrong.

"Without Deidra, there is no show," the director had told her matter-of-factly. "They weren't in love with the play; they were in love with her. You are no Deidra Shay."

Well, she was as good as Deidra—better in fact. She would bring this play back to life and bring Connor back to life, too. She knew it was too soon for Connor but why not sow the seed? He couldn't grieve forever, could he? And she relished the idea of being the new partner in what had become notorious romantic dalliances between Connor and Deidra.

Bethany was well aware that the other actors didn't like the way she had adopted the Deidra-kick at the end of the play. "It's not in the script—get your own signature or just bow and wave like the rest of us!" various cast members had told her. She had thought Connor would see it differently, but that had backfired. Obviously the "Deidra Kick" was seen as off limits by everyone. And Connor wouldn't even tell her where Deidra got those awesome panties that had pleased the crowd. Well, she would do the Deidra-kick; the audience expected it. But she planned to add something of her own—her very own. She would steal the show.

Fifteen minutes before curtain time, excited whispers could be heard from near the window, which overlooked Houston Street. With irritation, Bethany turned away from the mirror where she had been watching herself practice the facial expressions that carried her part throughout the show. What did they think they were doing? Everyone should be in character by now.

With her irritation came a wave of jealousy. Since Deidra's death, Bethany had become an outcast—was excluded from the supportive circle that Deidra had enjoyed in this group. As an understudy, she had never really been a part of things, but now she was the lead and was still left out of the close-knit theatre family. You'd think she'd killed Deidra herself! Not that she hadn't fantasized now and then, but that was show business, right? But if she said one word— one little word—about improving the role, you'd think she was blaspheming.

As Bethany drew closer to the window, she could hear excited snippets of conversation.

"Right there—by that lamp post!"

"I don't see her."

"You're imagining things."

"No! She waved at me!"

"Who?" Bethany strained to see who they were talking about but all she saw was the usual line of people waiting to get into the theatre. "Someone important?"

"Deidra!" Sandy told her. "She was on the other side of the street, and when she saw me looking at her she waved!"

Bethany couldn't keep the aggravation from showing on her face. "Oh for Pete's sake, get over it, will you?" Her thoughtless comment was met with total silence. She tried to soften her tone. "I know it's hard, but we have to accept that Deidra is gone." The last thing Bethany needed was for someone to intentionally screw up her lines because she wasn't still focusing on Deidra Shay.

"You go right ahead and accept it, Bethany. The rest of us miss her—as our friend and as the lead of this show."

Bethany couldn't miss the insult. She shook her head and walked away, but not before she threw her own verbal punch. "Maybe if someone other than me would focus on the show now it would be a lot better."

The play didn't go badly. Maybe it wasn't perfect, but most of the jokes drew laughs from the audience, and Bethany was pretty sure Connor, three rows up in the center of the house, had actually started the applause a couple of times. A pretty, tiny woman sat in the seat next to Connor, and Bethany was surprised to recognize Jesse. She remembered how cozy Connor and Jesse had gotten at Deidra's memorial service and wondered if he was more over Deidra than he was letting on. There was a moment during a difficult step in the tango when Bethany could have sworn she saw Deidra sitting next to him, and nearly lost her balance. Bethany's partner slipped his arm around her back and covered the move with a deep, floor sweeping dip. "Someone losing focus?" he had growled in her ear, too low for the audience to hear but loud enough for her to catch the reference to her earlier comment.

The ovation was adequate—not a standing, rowdy cheer but adequate. As the cast took their last bow and filed off, Bethany turned expertly, twirled to center stage and, giving the audience her most flirty, sexy grin, executed the Deidra-kick-and-flip. But she didn't show them black panties and a flashing red heart. What she had under her skirt was her naked-as-the-day-she-was-born ass with "The End" painted across it in bright red letters.

Just as she bent slightly forward to give the audience a clear-but-quick view of her bare butt, Bethany felt a push from behind and tripped. Her arms flailed wildly, but the four-inch heels weren't made for balance, and she fell forward. A surprised scream escaped her as her nose struck the wooden stage floor. Blood started pooling on the boards almost immediately, and a collective gasp went up from the crowd. An ice-cold burst of air blew her skirt up to her neck, leaving her struggling to pull it down while not only her bottom was exposed but everything else a pair of panties might cover.

Deidra drew her hand back to deliver a wide, freezing slap to that bare ass just as she was grabbed on all sides and pulled behind the now wildly blowing curtain at the back of the stage. Giggles surrounded her. She felt like she was being hugged by a dozen people.

"I've been tempted myself," a raspy female voice whispered in her ear, "but we don't do that here."

"Bethany is a bitch but she's a professional dancer! What the hell was that?" Connor growled.

"That was Deidra," Jesse said, and when he stared at her in shock she only nodded.

CHAPTER 21

There was a full column of Carpenters listed on Whitepages.com for Montrose, Pennsylvania. *A whole column*, Suzanne groaned, *and maybe not one who knows him*. But she couldn't think of anything else to do, and so she started making calls.

"Nope, sorry, Honey. You have the wrong number," the first person to answer told her with a slight quaver in her voice. Parkinson's? Stroke?

Of course I do, Suzanne thought, why couldn't his name be Gihizabub? Or Jellikins? Carpenter? It might as well be Jones or Smith! And then, to her surprise, the sweet voice on the other end of the line continued.

"That Brian is from a different Carpenter family altogether. He's Marilyn's boy, isn't he? Doesn't live with his mother any more, of course. An important

213

young man like that! But he takes good care of her, he does. Got her that lovely house on South Main Street. I'm sure she can tell you how to get a hold of him. Would you like me to get the number for you? It's right here in the book if you hold on a minute."

"No, no thank you. I can find it," Suzanne tried to hang up but the voice continued.

"Here it is. It's a good thing I looked it up, because Marilyn still has it under Floyd's name. Can't be too careful these days, you know. A lady might attract the wrong kind of person if she lists a number under her own name. Lets strangers know there isn't a man in the house, you know."

"You've been too kind," Suzanne assured her. "Thank you so very much."

"You tell Marilyn that Trudy says hello, you hear? And tell her I'm praying for her and Brian."

"I'll be sure to do that," Suzanne said and hung up before Trudy could ask her to relay any more messages to Marilyn. Thank God for small towns and trusting minds. Suzanne hadn't missed the fact that if she had been a man, the whole conversation might have gone differently.

"Mrs. Carpenter? My name is Suzanne. I'm friends with Brian and Jesse ..."

"Oh, thank heavens! I've tried and tried to call Jesse but she isn't answering her phone! Brian will think I did it on purpose! But of course she watched the news, didn't she? You'd think she'd have called me." The woman's voice went from strong to quavering to downright whiny in the space of thirty seconds, and Brian moved up several notches in Suzanne's opinion. Obviously Mrs. Carpenter could be a lot to deal with.

"Mrs. Carpenter, Jesse is out of town and asked me to try to reach Brian because she had to go to a meeting and hadn't been able to tell him." It wasn't entirely untrue, Suzanne told herself. Jesse certainly was in a meeting and apparently she wouldn't have been able to reach Brian if she had tried, but it had been on the news? "Mrs. Carpenter? What was on the news?"

"The accident, of course! Brian is a very important professional in this town. Channel 16 was here and everything. I'm sure Jesse saw it. Who did you say you are?"

"My name is Suzanne, and Jesse didn't see it because Jesse and I are in New York. What happened?"

"One of those terrible water trucks for the gas company. There is just too much traffic, and now look what they've done! My poor Brian; and what am I supposed to do if something happens to him? You would think that Jesse would at least call to offer me a ride to Community Medical Center but oh, no, she's just too busy to be bothered with ..."

Suzanne hung up the phone. She would apologize later, send flowers or a card to Mrs. Carpenter, but first she needed to find the news report. Was Montrose local news even posted online? And then she needed to call the Community Medical Center and get a status on Brian. Maybe, just maybe, she could pass as Mrs. Carpenter. Grinning, she started practicing her elderly-mother-voice as she searched for Montrose, PA on her iPhone. Channel 16 might have been there, but she couldn't find anything on their web site. Police blotter—that should tell her something.

When Deidra was a tiny, tiny girl and was her mother's only love, she would squirm to escape from her mother's embrace so she could go—somewhere. She didn't know where, exactly, but somewhere, anywhere, that she could belong. From the beginning, she knew she didn't belong at the Free Methodist Church quoting poems with the other children and listening to how dancing was a sin and roller skating was just dancing on wheels. She didn't belong in puffy flowered pastel dresses and Shirley Temple Ringlets.

Petite teenagers wore miniskirts and hip-hugging jeans, but Deidra wasn't petite. Her huge chest made boys stare, and that made her blush. She didn't belong in high school.

When the guidance counselor suggested her gift for writing and public speaking would make her an excellent English teacher, Deidra experienced such crushing disappointment she could barely speak. "I was thinking a writer or actress," she said softly.

The guidance counselor actually laughed. "That doesn't really happen," she said, "at least not here. Maybe if you lived in New York or Philadelphia, and you certainly don't want that, do you?"

Yes, yes! I do want that! Deidra thought, but she simply picked up her books and left the office, gasping for life like a fish out of water. She didn't live in New York or Philadelphia, and god knew she didn't belong in Montrose.

Deidra enrolled at the closest state university, "So you can come home every weekend and I can visit you," her mother had smiled happily. Deidra had wondered how she could get enough money to just run away. She suffered through one semester with a

Barbie-Doll freshman roommate who nearly cried when Deidra brought black accessories for the Barbie's lavender room, and who reported Deidra for smoking on the fire escape instead of going outside, which was the rule. Deidra didn't belong with Barbie Doll, so her mother got her a place of her own in exchange for Deidra not running away before the year was over.

When Deidra's friends walked her to that first audition and Jesse hugged her outside the auditorium, whispering, "Break a leg," Deidra found out what it was like to be sick with hope.

Deidra Shay stepped onto the university stage at the age of nineteen and, for the first time in her life, she belonged somewhere. She stood up straight; she laughed; she cried; she raged; she joked; she drew applause from the casting director; she was home.

The ghost of Deidra Shay found herself in the wings of the theatre on Houston Street in New York City and felt the weight of death fall from her shoulders. She had been moving desperately from one place to another, frantically searching in an escalating rage for her ever-after, and suddenly she was there—right where she belonged. She took a deep breath; she stood up straight; she laughed; she cried; she raged;

she joked; she relaxed into the welcoming warmth around her and surrendered.

"I remember her first blundering dance steps on this very stage," Agnes sighed. "Not a skilled stepper but a whole lot of talent. Great heart."

"Whitey, hold that curtain still. We'll scare away everyone but the weirdoes," a small woman in a big hat ordered the quiet white-haired man standing in the shadows. "That girl makes more wind than Carol did."

"No one makes more wind than I did," retorted a woman in a colorful caftan, sporting the longest cigarette holder Deidra had ever seen.

"You broke the law, you know. Haven't you heard that 'the show must go on'? You nearly destroyed it! Come with me and I'll help you learn the ropes," a low voice whispered in Deidra's ear and she turned to see one of the most handsome men she'd ever laid eyes on still holding her arm.

A beautiful blond woman took the arm being held by Mr. Gorgeous. "Leave her alone, Farley, you old wolf. Honey, you just messed up the play. If she tries to be you she isn't going to get far anyway. Don't sweat the small stuff. A little joke here and there won't hurt though," and the woman raised her eyebrows in such a suggestive manner that Deidra had to laugh.

"Listen to Natasha. She knows," a young girl chimed in. The voices were all around her, male and female, high and low, and she started to recognize them, or thought she did. "Are you …" she began, and a pull so strong it lifted her right off the stage and into the spinning darkness took her by surprise.

She could hear exclamations of surprise and dismay behind her. In front of her, she could feel that pull and hear her name being called over and over again. She was spinning out of control, with tears pouring down her face and frustration battering her as she was sucked into the ring.

Suzanne could get to Scranton in three hours by car, four hours by bus and couldn't get there at all by train. Pretty out of the way place in her opinion, and she wondered again why anyone chose northeastern Pennsylvania as a place to live. Visit she could understand, but live? It wasn't connected to anywhere!

She was exhausted from the last few days and was about to buy a bus ticket when it dawned on her that Scranton might not have taxis in the middle of the night and there may not be bus service back until tomorrow. There was only one way to prove what had happened to Brian and that was to go see for herself.

She had found out that Montrose did, indeed, have a newspaper, but it wouldn't be out until Wednesday. Channel 16 might very well have collected information, but they didn't have any available yet; maybe by time they did the eleven o'clock news. Nothing was posted on the police blotter online, either, although she might have been able to get information from the Montrose police if anyone had answered the phone. She didn't think there would even be a Jesse if she waited; just Jesse's body giving Deidra a place to live.

Half an hour later, a red Miata sped across the George Washington Bridge. The Boss was screaming from the CD player, the thermos was full of Columbian coffee and the driver was feeling every bit like a cowboy in a white hat.

The neurosurgeon sat hunched over a small desk in the Intensive Care Unit and reviewed his patient's records. "Let me know when the intracranial pressure stabilizes. I don't want to continue therapeutic coma any longer than necessary."

"Yes, doctor." The intravenous bag dripped, dripped, dripped, making sure Brian Carpenter continued to sleep.

Deidra's ring sat on the table between them. They hadn't discussed where they would go after Bethany's disastrous bow, but neither of them was ready to face the intimacy of Connor's apartment. He simply pulled open the door of a bar without even looking at the name, and Jesse walked into the dark room and took a seat at a window table. Connor put the ring in the middle of the table and went to get two Scotch and waters.

"So," Connor drank half of his drink in one gulp and then stared into it as he turned the glass around and around, "if we do this—call Deidra—do I get to see her?"

Jesse shrugged. "I haven't seen her since the night before the memorial service. Maybe she doesn't feel the need to be seen now that she's figured out how to move stuff around, including me." Jesse was shocked to realize that she didn't really care anymore. She had lost her best friend. She had lost the love of her life. She had lost her right to her own mind and body. There didn't seem to be anything else to lose.

Connor sighed and took another sip. "But I don't want to see you acting like Deidra. I want to see Deidra."

Jesse's face remained blank. "If you think you have any say in the matter, you're dead wrong. I can't even say for sure if Deidra has a say in it. I don't think she has a lot of control or she wouldn't be making one-word statements on Facebook. Deidra loved to talk." The memory of Deidra's constant chatter surprised a smile out of Jesse.

Connor saw the smile and softened, his own lips curving up in memory. "She could tell the truth or a lie and make either one a good story. So, okay, do we sit in the dark or light candles, or what?"

"Connor, I've honestly never called her on purpose. I do know that when I've seen her it's been in the middle of the night when I was sleeping or dreaming, and that neither Suzanne nor Brian ever saw Deidra. They saw curtains blow, pictures spin off the walls, drawers pop in and out, furniture move, messages appear on Facebook and me not only dancing but actually ordering Brian to have sex with me, or her, or whatever. She actually said, 'Fuck me. I want to feel again.' I don't think Deidra can actually feel physical touch without going through me. "

Connor raised his eyebrows. "Jesse, do you even say 'fuck' ?"

Jesse couldn't help but laugh. "Honestly? I might if I'm hurt or angry, but in reference to having sex? No. I don't. Is it that obvious?"

"Sort of." Connor reached across the table to pat her hand. "When I'm over Deidra, if I'm ever over Deidra, I think I want someone who never says 'fuck'."

"You'd die of boredom," Jesse said, and lifted her glass in a salute.

Connor watched Jesse's tiny hand lift the glass of Scotch to her lips and realized the ring he had bought for Deidra would never look good there.

His memory watched a long, slender hand, the finger nails matching the deep burgundy of her wine, as Deidra saluted him. He could see the diamond flash as they toasted their engagement, laughing in the back of the cab, Deidra's full red lips moving from laugh to smile to tease; her head dipping to his lap to place a suggestive mesmerizing kiss on the zipper of his dress pants. He could hear her laugh, deep and throaty; see her head suddenly fling back, her black hair whipping away from her face as she shook it—a wild mane. He heard Deidra laugh. He saw her sling one long, fishnet-stockinged leg over his thighs, felt the weight of her as she climbed into his lap; felt her tongue tease that sensitive nerve under his ear and felt the heat as he buried his face between her warm, musky breasts.

Connor threw both hands over his eyes, tasted the salt of his tears, and yearned. "God!" he cried. "What is life now?"

At that same moment, Jesse saw the long, trailing fingers sweeping ever so slightly along the floor of the train; saw again that diamond as she had seen it first, sparking in the lights of the station. Saw the disheveled curls tumbling, tumbling, tumbling as Deidra's head fell forward and Jesse knew—with a heart that screamed silently in darkness—knew Deidra was gone. She yearned. What other word was there for this? Her heart pulsed against her chest bone until Jesse wondered how and if she was ever going to breathe again.

At that moment—that exact moment—as Jesse and Connor faced their grief together, Deidra was pulled from the theatre into the ring and into their joined hands.

Jesse and Connor did not have to discuss the fact that Deidra was there. Her energy hummed between them, a wire pulled taut and vibrating. They didn't leave the table or even think about what was happening. They knew the second Deidra arrived and they gratefully embraced her presence.

CHAPTER 22

The three friends, Deidra, Connor and Jesse, sat in silence. Tears slid down their faces and dripped to the table. Every now and again someone passing on the sidewalk outside glimpsed through the window and turned quickly away. They couldn't bear the pain of the three people so evidently captured in mutual grief too private to gawk at or to share.

They finally left to wander through the city. They traced Deidra's life, starting on East 6th, where she had shared a jungle of rooms with six friends. From there they walked three blocks to her favorite coffee shop; even at this late hour, couples and individuals dressed in everything from formal wear to black slips and sandals sat at small tables on the sidewalk and drank coffee from huge ceramic mugs. The smell of cinnamon permeated the air. Connor stopped to get two steaming cups to go. Jesse invited Deidra to slip inside for a moment so she, too, could have a taste.

Arm in arm, they walked up Broadway to the theatre district and turned right to stand in tribute under the Barrymore Theatre awning. Deidra touched the marquee gently and laid her head against it. Her name would never be there now. A sob escaped Jesse, and Connor slipped his arm around her waist. So much was lost.

They had hot dogs at Frankie's, then walked the few blocks to old theatre row. Deidra had performed there in "The Tempest" one summer night long ago during Shakespeare on the Sidewalk. Now she scaled the wall of the courtyard and took on the guise of a siren once again. Just as it had on that magical night long ago, her gossamer gown caught in the wind and flew around her. Connor caught his breath.

This was Deidra's town. She took them to a club where they danced, at first encircling each other to sway gently to the music, then gyrating wildly to a hip-hop beat. Deidra laughed out loud as she twirled around the floor, her arms held out from her sides like wings as she flew. She grabbed Jesse's hand and spun her around, the two of them laughing together. Connor watched and applauded and kissed each of them when they returned, heated and glowing, from the dance floor. Deidra's diamond flashed in the artificial light. Connor was surprised to discover it was no longer in his pocket when Deidra was visible; she wore it.

They caught a cab to Brooklyn Bridge Park and walked along the river, huddled together on the pier to gaze at the Manhattan skyline, surprised all over again by the absence of the Twin Towers. Deidra knew that there would be many people like her living there if she ever cared to find them.

Now and then, Deidra would tease Jesse or Connor with her new skills. They passed an artistic display in a gallery window made up of hundreds of little girl's christening dresses, starched and standing in rows. Deidra set them spinning, hundreds of little dresses dancing as if they were still being worn. "Put them back!" Jesse insisted, "They'll be trying to arrest someone!" but Deidra giggled and let them fall in various postures, leaving them there to be a mystery.

Even in New York, certain places aren't open all night: museums, libraries, theatres. "This is the world of the vampire," Deidra hissed and bared her

229

teeth suggestively. "Do you remember my vampire days, Jesse?" Just like that, Deidra was dressed all in black, including her lips and nails. Her shoulders slumped, her chest drooped and she was the Goth chick that Jesse had first met in college orientation.

"You've come a long way, baby!" Jesse laughed but Connor looked confused. He had never known that Deidra. For the first time it dawned on him that he might have had a future with Deidra but it was Jesse who shared her past; now that was all there was ever going to be. He was surprised at the jealousy that flashed through him, the resentment. He wanted this time with Deidra, but it was Jesse who was sharing, laughing, remembering.

As if she knew what he was thinking, Deidra changed course and headed back to Houston Street. She transformed from the gawky college freshman to the beautiful actress, slipping her hand into Jesse's to gently brush Connor's cheek, nestle against his neck and reenact their engagement. Anyone watching would have seen the huge man swinging a tall, voluptuous woman one minute and a tiny wisp of a girl the next. Jesse gave herself to Deidra and allowed herself to be pulled away into that last glorious night.

The taxi driver who picked up a man and woman outside the theatre saw three people in the back seat of his cab but glanced in his mirror again to find only the two he had picked up in the first place. Down another street and the rear view mirror showed the same man but a small woman; again it was some kind of mind twitch as he took another glance to see the man and voluptuous brunette he had picked up doing things he could only hope someone would do with him someday. He shook his head firmly and made up his mind to get a full twelve hours of sleep before getting into the cab again. Obviously, he was seeing things.

At Port Authority, Deidra led Connor and Jesse down the steps and through the tunnels to the Martz Trailways bus depot. She flashed her ring to the imaginary everyone, although the last bus had gone, and covered Connor's mouth with the same passionate kiss she had given him then—that last second he had seen her.

Connor crumpled to the floor. He held the long fingers to his cheek, kissing them over and over again. "Please, please don't get on the bus."

Deidra knelt beside him and pulled him close, her breath soft and warm in his ear. Then she was gone, and all that was left was Jesse, crying softly in his arms. He leaned over to kiss the top of her head and for a moment he found himself wondering who he was kissing. There was something earth shattering about a woman who would give herself willingly to a friend the way Jesse was giving herself to Deidra, and so to him.

Connor and Jesse rode the subway to Connor's apartment in silence. They didn't know if Deidra was there or not. Certainly, she wasn't fully present like she had been for the past few hours. Her ring felt heavy in Connor's pocket. Wherever she was, she was no longer wearing it.

"Is she coming back? Is this what it's always like when you see her?"

Jesse blinked back tears. "It's never been like this. I think the two of us give her substance. We love her; we believe in her; we want her with us. But I think she gets tired, too. She draws from me and I draw from her. We burn each other out—or that's what it feels like. You have no idea how exhausted I am and have been." Jesse shook her head and smiled at him. "At least this time it was nice to visit with her. The other times I was surprised and sometimes terrified."

"It was the greatest gift you could have given us, Jesse. Thank you."

"You're welcome."

Connor didn't realize that Jesse was asleep until he felt her head fall against his shoulder. For the first time, he really studied her face and saw the dark circles under her eyes; the way her mouth seemed to pull down in her sleep. The subway lurched, and he had to grab her or she would have fallen into the aisle, and he was pretty sure she wouldn't have woken up. He remembered her saying, "You have no idea how exhausted I am and have been," and Suzanne's adamant, "No!", when he had first suggested that Jesse channel Deidra for him. The first stirring of guilt woke in his conscience; his arms encircled Jesse as she slept, pulling her closer.

She didn't wake up when they reached their stop. Connor wound up lifting her and carrying her to the curb where he flagged a taxi down. The driver carefully looked away as Connor settled Jesse's body into the seat next to him. Connor grinned, knowing the driver was probably wondering if she was dead or if Connor had slipped her something. He started to explain and stopped; it just didn't make a difference.

Let the guy have a story to tell when he went home that night.

At his apartment, Connor tried again without success to wake Jesse up. She was unconscious to the point that Connor was seriously worried. Silently, he cursed Suzanne for not giving him a little more information on what could happen if Jesse let Deidra in. Where was she anyway? If Suzanne had been so god-awful worried, why the hell had she left?

Carrying Jesse up the steps to his building was shockingly easy. Even in her velvet duster and evening dress, she was nearly weightless. Guilt bit at him again. He was sure Jesse hadn't been this thin when he had first met her.

Deidra watched Connor carry Jesse from the subway to the taxi, from the taxi to the apartment. She, too, saw the deep shadows under Jesse's eyes, the sorrow on her face, the loose fit of her dress. Jesse gave herself out of love, and out of love Deidra knew she had to stop accepting Jesse's gift.

Connor shifted Jesse slightly to get the key out of his pocket without having to lay her limp body down. Just as he was about to give it up as impossible, Deidra opened the door and helped him carry Jesse inside.

"Glad you're still here," he said, and Deidra was silent.

While Connor was wondering where Suzanne was, she was wondering the same. The trip to Scranton from New York was easy—straight across the George Washington onto Route 80, keep going straight into Pennsylvania, take 380 North to 84 West to Scranton. No problem.

Finding the hospital wasn't as easy but it wasn't bad either, thanks to her GPS. Getting into the ICU was another matter. She had called patient information to find out where he was. Knowing how difficult it was to get information over the phone with the new HIPPA regulations she didn't even try, figuring she would do better just showing up.

At the ICU unit, she watched as visitors for other patients quietly walked through the double doors and followed them, trying to look confident. It might have worked if she hadn't had to stop and read names as she went. A helpful, annoying aide saw her. "Can I help you?"

"Brian Carpenter?"

"His mother said he wouldn't be having any more visitors."

"She never expected me to make the trip all the way from Philadelphia tonight, but I just couldn't stand not seeing for myself. You understand, I'm sure."

The aide nodded and led Suzanne to Brian's bed, and Suzanne was grateful she had. Brian's face was so swollen she wouldn't have recognized him. No wonder he wasn't in Montrose! The shock and grief on her face must have convinced the aide because she patted Suzanne's arm and whispered, "I'm so sorry," before she went about her duties.

Suzanne didn't know what she had expected. Maybe tell Brian that Jesse thought he'd left her and get him to call or write something? This Brian wasn't going to say or write anything. His face was so distorted that Suzanne didn't even know if Jesse would believe it was him if Suzanne sent a picture to her cell phone. The sign said, "No cell phones allowed," which she was pretty sure included her.

Still, the little "beep-beep-beep" from the machine over Brian's bed was steady, nothing strange was going on in the squiggle lines across the monitor and the aide who had brought her here had walked away after one quick glance, so he must be doing okay. Suzanne slipped her cell phone out of her pocket and selected camera just as a nurse walked into the room.

"Excuse me, Miss. That's not allowed," she said briskly just as Suzanne snapped a picture of the man she had been assured was Brian. "You can't take pictures." The stern nurse didn't know what to do when Suzanne simply turned and walked past her out of the room. "Excuse me," the nurse called after her but Suzanne just kept going, down the hall and through the elevator doors. Jesse would just have to believe that this was, indeed, Brian. It certainly explained why he hadn't called.

Once in her car, Suzanne attached the photo with the caption, "This is Brian. Call me," and sent it to Jesse's phone. With disgust she saw that the message wasn't going anywhere. She tried calling Jesse but the call went straight to voice mail. Jesse must have her phone turned off. The play; of course she had it off. Frustrated, Suzanne simply said, "Call me ASAP," to the answering machine and headed out of town.

Fifteen minutes later, she saw a sign for Mount Pocono and a huge white wall which turned out to be the thickest, whitest, scariest bank of cloud Suzanne had ever encountered. She had no idea if she was on the road or the shoulder or if there were cars in front of her or in back of her. Slowing her car to a crawl, she gradually pulled to the right, praying there was a gravel shoulder that would tell her when she was off the highway. There was. Suzanne genuflected in thanks to whatever god wanted to take credit for getting her stopped without running over a cliff, turned on her emergency blinkers and settled in for the night. Hopefully Jesse would get her message, because Suzanne wasn't going anywhere.

The sun wasn't up yet. Connor was sure he had just drifted off when he felt Jesse slip out of bed. She had been so exhausted he truly hadn't expected to see her open her eyes before sometime in the afternoon. He could hear her soft laughter; hear her feet moving in rhythm across the floor.

Connor flipped on his bedside lamp and stared. Jesse still wearing the lace panties and bra he had stripped her down to before tucking her into bed stood in the middle of the room. Her head was tilted back, and a flirtatious smile turned the corners of her mouth up. Her head moved back and forth gracefully, causing her hair to slide across the bare skin of her shoulders. Her arms were raised and her hips swayed as she did a slow cha-cha. Suddenly her leg kicked gracefully and she turned, lowering her head to her shoulder as she danced in a new direction.

Connor had seen Deidra dance countless times. He recognized her even as she used Jesse's body to perform. All night he had watched Jesse and Deidra slide back and forth in his vision, but this wasn't Deidra coming and going; this was Deidra fully encased in Jesse, using her body as she had her own.

Since Deidra's death, all Connor had wanted was to hold her one more time, love her one more time, say good-bye. He had dreamed of her heat. He had walked around in her robe just to smell her perfume and her sweat. He had offered to sell his soul a million times for just one more moment in her arms, crushed against her breast, their bodies merged in passion.

When Jesse and Suzanne convinced him that Deidra really and truly possessed Jesse, he had seen a way to get his one wish; had even planned on using Jesse to hold Deidra one more time. Last night he had decided that he couldn't. He had seen Jesse's exhaustion, her generous spirit, her beauty and what he hadn't wanted to admit to himself was that he had seen, for the first time since Deidra's death, the possibility of a future. Jesse had shown him that he might still have a heart; he might be able to love again.

Now here was Jesse as Deidra, and his will fell apart. "The road to hell is paved with good intentions," he said softly, and gave himself up to Deidra's dance and his own overwhelming desire.

A soft wind swept through the room even though the windows were closed. A blown curtain drifted across Connor's body, fingers of seduction. He closed his eyes and let Deidra whisper to him, let her lips touch his neck with feather softness. Her fingers grazed his cheeks, ran along his eyes and over his mouth. He could feel the tips of her breasts just tease his own chest, then slide down to his navel. He groaned in ecstasy and pain.

Deidra's voice, throaty and inviting, said his name, over and over again. "Connor, touch me. Touch me." Her breath grew sharper, faster, and his sped up with her until she grasped a hold of him. "Fuck me, Connor," she invited, and just as he put his hands around her hips and drew her to him, he heard another voice.

Jesse, manipulated in her sleep, whimpered, "No. Please, no," and Connor opened his eyes.

For one moment Deidra's lidded eyes, full of invitation and desire, gave way to Jesse's blank dream-stare. Deidra's demanding whispers and promises were silenced by Jesse's pleas, and Connor was undone.

Deidra was back, touching, begging, pleading, but Connor backed away. "Don't, Deidra," he begged and when she wouldn't stop he pushed her away. "Jesus Christ, look at her!" he demanded.

Deidra stepped out of Jesse's body and watched as Jesse slumped to the floor, now naked and still half asleep. Even in her dream world she whimpered, her body shuddering in the wind Deidra generated. Jesse was a rag doll on the rug.

In his anger Connor turned to Deidra. "It's rape!" he started to scream, and then stopped.

In the first streaks of morning he saw Deidra kneel by Jesse and put her arms around Jesse's shivering form. Then Deidra lay down at Jesse's side and rocked her tenderly back and forth. Connor drew a blanket from the bed and Deidra took it and carefully wrapped it around Jesse and both Connor and Deidra watched as Jesse relaxed and smiled gently. "Deidra," she said softly.

"Jesse," Deidra answered.

Jesse's small hand reached out to grasp Deidra's long fingers. "I love you, Deidra."

"I love you, too, Jesse," Deidra said, "Thank you."

Connor shivered on the bed as Jesse smiled in her sleep and Deidra faded away.

CHAPTER 23

Suzanne woke up to fog, fog and more fog, and to a police officer tapping on her window. "Turn on your lights and pull into line. Stay close enough to follow the lights in front of you. The cloud bank disperses before you get to Route 80. This is a caravan. Absolutely do not pass, and stay alert for brake lights. Let's go." She had been rescued.

Jesse slept. She didn't see the sun shine through the window. She didn't hear Connor get up to use the bathroom or know that he closed the blinds to shield her eyes. She didn't feel his arms go around her and hold her warm and secure. She just slept.

Connor didn't know for sure where fantasy ended and reality started, and he didn't actually care. For the first time in weeks, he wasn't hung over. He made sure the alarm, both his and Jesse's cell phones, the land line and the doorbell were disabled or turned off. He tiptoed to the table and started organizing information on the new play. If she woke up and was afraid or worried, he wanted to be there to take care of her.

Deidra curled inside the ring and reviewed everything that had happened to her since getting on the bus what now seemed like forever ago. She thought about her mother, the service, the crows, the theatre, Suzanne, the bus driver, her teacher, Bethany and the spirits of the theatre. She thought about Connor and how much she hated to let him go and how much she needed to. She thought about Jesse crumpled and exhausted. Deidra knew what she was going to do and she needed Jesse to help her just one last time.

Deidra turned on Connor's laptop and found Facebook. "What's on your mind?" it asked.

"Theatre," Deidra posted.

Connor was reading at the table when Jesse finally woke up in the early afternoon. He looked more like a college professor and less like a lumber jack, with reading glasses perched half-way down his nose and books and papers spread out around him.

Jesse watched him from her nest in the covers, trying to put together pieces of the night before. By now she knew that she probably wouldn't remember everything. When Deidra took over her body she often took over her mind, too. Jesse felt the sheets slide across her body and wondered if Deidra had made love to Connor. She was surprised to find out she hoped so. She had lost any sense of being herself or having choices where Deidra was concerned. She just wanted Deidra to be happy.

As if he could feel her eyes on him, Connor raised his head. "Coffee?" he asked, and Jesse nodded. She had to admire a man that could act like nothing had happened after spending the entire night with a ghost and waking up next to a naked woman he barely knew.

She could remember enough of the night before to feel shy. If there was more, she wasn't sure she wanted to know right now. "If I have clothes I think I'd like to go to the hotel."

He poured a cup of coffee for her anyway. "Your clothes are hanging in the bathroom." He stepped into the small kitchen space. She was grateful, sure he was giving her some privacy to get out of bed. Deidra had shown good taste in picking this guy.

Connor was gone when she came out of the bathroom. She gathered her purse and coat and headed for the hotel. She expected to find Suzanne. She wasn't sure what to make of the fact that Suzanne had disappeared yesterday afternoon and hadn't been heard from since. A wave of dizziness washed over her and she decided to take a long bath and then sort things out.

Suzanne heard the water running when she finally got to the hotel. She planned on closing her eyes until Jesse came out. Hours later she was still asleep, fully clothed, lying cross-ways on the bed.

At dusk, the phone in their room rang insistently, pulling Suzanne to consciousness. Jesse, still wrapped in a towel, blinked awake in the other bed. "Hello?" she murmured without even picking up the receiver.

Suzanne answered the phone, struggling to focus. "Get up. Deidra wants us at the theatre," Connor ordered, and the line went dead. It struck Suzanne that she didn't even think that was strange. How was she ever going to explain that a ghost gave orders and she not only believed but accepted that as normal?

They met in the lobby and walked to Houston Street. The days were getting longer, and Jesse was thankful for the warmth in the air. She was always cold now, as if her blood was drying up and blowing away. Sometimes she wondered if she could die from being cold. At one point, she lagged behind, too exhausted to keep up, until Suzanne took one arm and Connor took the other to support her. "We need a cab," Suzanne told Connor over Jesse's head, but Jesse interrupted.

"I want to walk. I think it helps." They didn't ask her what it helped with. They could both see she was weaker every time she shared herself with Deidra.

There was tension among the actors inside the theatre as tickets were sold and the stage was set up. The previous night's poor performance had received scathing remarks online, and the play was fighting for its life.

From behind the curtain, Bethany watched in fear. She couldn't shake the memory of seeing Deidra sitting in the audience the night before, whether it had really happened or not. She had spent all night and day revisiting the script, finding her own character and style. Another night of failing miserably would get her removed from the play altogether, and she knew it.

When the house lights came down, Bethany surprised her audience by entering not in the bawdy burlesque style of Deidra Shay, but rather with a villainous sensuality that exuded a not-so-hidden evil. She mixed a cool, aloof delivery of lines with an inside-joke smirk to her audience, as if she and they were complicit and the man she was seducing on stage was the innocent victim of the entire house. Gradually, the audience bought it. Finally, they were laughing out loud at her shenanigans, and she rewarded them with an impish grin. Jesse glanced at Connor and saw him smiling and nodding his approval.

The dance scenes were the same. Jesse held her breath, remembering Bethany's nearly disastrous trip the night before—one she was fairly certain Deidra had instigated. A slight movement in the curtain drew her attention and she was shocked to see Deidra there, watching the play. She nudged Connor and turned toward him only to see that he was already focused on the same curtain. Glancing to her other side, Jesse saw Suzanne sitting wide-eyed and mesmerized. Suzanne hadn't seen Deidra at any other time since her death, but she saw her now.

Then it happened; at the point where Bethany had stumbled the night before she hesitated as if unsure of herself. Suddenly Deidra was there, on stage, dancing next to her. She didn't touch her or join with her. She simply danced. And Bethany, as if she could feel Deidra there, followed.

"What's she doing?" Suzanne hissed.

"She's helping her," Jesse replied, and Connor nodded.

For the remainder of the play, they watched the curtains, catching a movement every now and then, or a flash of Deidra's smile, her extended arm, her foot keeping time. Bethany was doing one hell of a job, and Deidra was cheering her on.

As the grand finale got closer, Jesse could feel Connor stiffen next to her. Would Bethany attempt the Deidra-flip-n-kick again? If she tried, would Deidra let her do it? And then the audience was applauding and the actors were taking bows. When it was time for Bethany to come out, she didn't appear. The entire audience grew quiet and stared at the side curtain where she should have been. For that second, Jesse honestly hoped Bethany wasn't dead or badly maimed.

And then, obviously on cue, the orchestra struck a new chord and Bethany walked to center stage, her arms draped through those of her leading man and another actor who had been seduced earlier in the play. She wore a floor-length white satin form-fitting gown, over the elbow white gloves and sequined heels. Her hair was swept into a sophisticated up-do, and one hand carried the longest, most outrageous cigarette holder Jesse had ever seen. The men were in black tuxedos and top hats and carried canes. They tipped their hats to the audience, twirled Bethany between them, and somehow she wound up facing the stage as the men faced the audience. In one coordinated, elegant movement, they caught the hem of her gown and lifted it, exposing a red thong and the words, "The End," on Bethany's perfectly muscled behind. At that moment, she turned to look at the audience over her shoulder and winked.

It was only a flash, held just long enough for the message to be read, and the lovely gown was back in place and Bethany and her escorts joined the other actors for a group bow. In the wings, smiling as if she had planned it herself, Deidra Shay glimmered among the curtains and applauded.

Jesse started to cry.

CHAPTER 24

They sat in their chairs while the house lights came up and the audience filtered out. Crew members clearing the stage started to ask them to leave but, seeing that it was Connor, simply went about their business. When the building was empty, the theatre manager came quietly up behind them to touch Connor respectfully on the shoulder. "It's locked. Pull the door closed behind you." Connor nodded.

Still they sat. Deidra had a reason for wanting them here, and they would wait until whatever was going to happen had happened. They knew they could call her. They knew they could make her come to them. Connor took the ring out of his pocket and held it in his palm, studying it. Was Deidra there? Or was she somewhere among the shadows? A breeze lifted a stage curtain briefly and Connor turned to it expectantly but then it was still.

"You know her better than anyone else, Jesse. Is she coming?" Connor whispered. Jesse simply nodded.

The first sign that Deidra was with them came as a tug on the ring in Connor's hand. Instinctively he closed his fingers around it and held on. "Let me go," Deidra's voice sighed. Connor wasn't sure he'd really heard it but then it came again, louder. "Let me go," Deidra said. This time there was a touch of pleading in her tone.

I don't think I can, Connor thought. He made his fingers loosen but at the last minute Jesse grabbed the ring from him and clutched it against her chest.

"No!" she said loudly. "No, Deidra, No! Don't leave me."

A soft wind started its course around the theatre, a ripple starting at one end of the stage and running to the other. In the wind, a sigh barely loud enough to be heard was repeated over and over again. Then Deidra was there, not solid like the night before but rather a mixture of film and fog shimmering in front of them.

"Deidra," Jesse reached to trace the line of Deidra's face, "I can't bear to lose you."

"Home," Deidra said. "Home."

"Home is with me!" Jesse was nearing hysteria. "You can't choose this over me! You can't!"

"Please," Deidra begged again. "Home."

Suzanne kept her eyes on the shimmer that was Deidra and slipped her arm around Jesse's waist. "Jesse, honey, you're exhausted and sick. Deidra is setting you free. Can't you see that? This is her light at the end of the tunnel. Come on. She's letting you go. Do the same for her."

Suzanne looked at Connor and realized he wasn't going to be any help. Slack-jawed and hypnotized, he stared at Deidra and shivered slightly. Next to him, Jesse also shivered, caught up in the frigid air that followed Deidra everywhere. At that moment, Suzanne knew why she was here; why Deidra had included her. She and she alone had been able to tell Deidra to stop. She had interacted with but not been affected by Deidra multiple times. The ring didn't mesmerize her or even make her cold.

Suzanne was the ticket to freedom for all of them. She could let Deidra go and, when she did, she knew she would also be saving Jesse. But it was going

253

to hurt. She couldn't even imagine how much it was going to hurt Jesse to really let Deidra pass into another world. They had become so linked that Suzanne wasn't sure Jesse's mind could take another loss. Suzanne looked at Jesse's thin frame, her bones already protruding from her jaw and cheeks in so little time. How much longer before Deidra had absorbed every bit of energy Jesse had? Suddenly it was very clear to Suzanne that, as dangerous as the separation might be now, it would be much more dangerous later.

"Give me the ring, Jesse," Suzanne said softly. She held out her hand.

Jesse shook her head no and continued to stare at Deidra.

Changing tactics, Suzanne held out her hand to Deidra and was surprised when Deidra put her hand into Suzanne's. "It's Deidra's ring, Jesse. See how her finger is so bare without it? Give her the ring, Jesse. She wants it back."

Deidra continued to hold out her hand. Slowly, as if in a trance, Jesse opened her fingers. Suzanne held her breath and watched as Jesse held the ring out to Deidra, then slipped it onto the waiting finger.

Deidra stepped close to Connor, took his face between her hands and kissed him. Suzanne felt tears gush down her own face as Connor captured Deidra's hands and buried his face in them. For a second, Suzanne was afraid he would grab the ring and not let her go after all. Later, much later, he would confess that he had desperately wanted to do just that.

Next, Deidra stepped to Jesse. It was impossible to see where one started and the other ended as they embraced; they had become so comfortable sharing a mutual space. Suzanne could see Deidra force herself to leave Jesse. "I can live here," she explained. "Jesse, with you I can only come and go in your life but here I have a life of my own. And I'm hurting you—I can see it. Oh, Jesse, please ..." They touched foreheads and stood together, entwined, and Suzanne found herself hoping she never loved anyone as much as Deidra and Jesse loved each other. It was far too painful.

Finally, Deidra turned to Suzanne and smiled. "Thank you," she said. Her long fingers reached toward Suzanne, the ring sparkling in the low light, but before they reached her, Deidra was gone.

A year after Deidra's death Jesse and Mary hosted a gathering of friends and relatives at the Summer House Grill. The walls were covered with pictures of Deidra's life, from her first day of birth to the last character portrait from "Achilles Heel".

"A Celebration of Deidra's Life," the invitations had read, and the guests took it seriously, showing up in bright spring colors, outlandish hats and brightly painted nails. The guests overflowed into the street, until South Main looked like an explosion of brightly colored flowers.

Jesse raised her eyebrows when Suzanne showed up escorting Tonya, her tango partner from the year before. "What can I say," Suzanne shrugged. "I went back to visit Deidra a few times and look who I ran into."

"How's Deidra doing?" Brian asked and was nearly knocked over when Suzanne threw her arms around him in an exuberant hug.

"She's fine! Becoming a first-class legend—but how are you?" Suzanne stood back and checked him over from head to toe until his face turned red. He waved her off with a threatened hit from his cane.

"Still talking backwards occasionally, but not as often as I used to. Jesse says I talk too well, actually, so I guess I'm healing."

Jesse went to greet Sal, but Brian lingered next to Suzanne. "I never thanked you," he said softly.

"Thank you for believing in me and," he grinned, "for breaking into the ICU for that picture. Wish I'd been awake enough to see you do it."

Suzanne's eyes opened wide. "Holy shit! Is that who I think it is?"

"Where?" Brian looked around, puzzled.

"Connor brought Bethany with him! Honest to God, Deidra must be livid!"

"I hope not or we better find cover," Brian replied.

Nothing ruined the day. By that evening, Suzanne could only surmise that Deidra had found her own happiness wherever she was. Throughout the day, she had watched Jesse's face shift from happiness to sorrow as memories were found and shared, but all in all she looked good. There was no reason to put off the trip she and Tonya had planned. They skipped out early.

When everyone was gone or settled into the various hotels and inns, Brian quietly stole out to Jesse's front porch, where he knew he would find her. She stood alone in the moonlight, gazing down at Berry Street.

He moved up close behind her, slipping his arms around her waist and enjoying the way she leaned back into him. "Any one moving around down there?" he asked.

"Not right now, or at least not that I can see."

"Maybe you could see them better with this," he said. He pulled a package out from under the wicker chair where he had hidden it earlier and handed it to her.

"What's this for?"

"Because I love you and I want you to do what you love doing."

Jesse yanked at the ribbon impatiently, revealing not one but two boxes taped together. She raised a questioning eye and he couldn't stop himself from kissing her. He didn't think he would ever be able to get that close to her again without kissing her.

"Let's see," he held the first box out to her, "it had the highest rating, but you can exchange it if you want to. I mean—digital is the best for catching orbs and other things, right? How many people can take pictures of ghosts, and here you are a natural. Suzanne writes, you take pictures, I invest money—sounds like a great book venture to me, don't you think?"

"Brian ..."

"I'm not done. This other one is a Honeywell Pentax Spotmatic. I had to buy five of them before I got one that actually works. They're getting pretty scarce, you know. Anyway—isn't this the fully manual one you need if you want to take pictures of something besides ghosts? "

"Brian…."

"Someone told me that you're an artist," he said. "They said you take pictures."

She kissed him, carefully put the cameras down, and kissed him again.

"Does that mean you like them?"

And she kissed him one more time for good luck.

ABOUT THE AUTHOR

Regge Episale holds a BA from Binghamton University SUNY and an MFA in writing from Hollins University. Her first poem was published when she was ten years old and she has been writing ever since. Some of her favorite memories include listening to members of her family talk about ghosts and their own experiences with the paranormal.

She has two children and two grandchildren, whom she adores and sees as often as possible. Her favorite color is red; her hobbies include writing, singing, painting and playing the piano. And yes—she absolutely does believe in ghosts.